Mistletoe Misconduct

Mistletoe Misconduct

Have yourself a very smutty little holiday season.

GN ♡♡♡

Copy/Line edits by Cassidy Hudspeth

Proofreading by Louise Murphy (Kat's Literary Services)

Illustrated cover art and internal character illustrations by Elena Bushe (ElenBushe_Art on Instagram)

Cover typography by Samantha Randolph (SamsCreativeCure on Instagram)

Internal formatting by me, done via Atticus

Contents

Also by

<u>Philia Players Series</u>
Quiver
Tremble
Quake
Book #4 in the Philia Players Series: Coming Soon!
Sign up for my newsletter for a sneak peek at Luca
and Samara's story.
<u>Secret Trials Series</u>
Professional rugby (rugby thighs and hoochie daddy
shorts? Sign me up!) x Female college soccer series
COMING SOON!
<u>Rosa Ranch Series</u>
Western romance with cowboys and a lot of Latin
influence COMING SOON!
<u>Standalones & Novellas</u>
Mistletoe Misconduct

Content Warning

There are mentions of family trauma, a parent with a mental illness (schizophrenia), an MC with well-controlled schizophrenia, an MC with chronic migraines and an on-page migraine, feelings of unworthiness, sex work, terminally ill children and children undergoing cancer treatment, a dysfunctional childhood, explicit language, and lots of consensual and sometimes rough intercourse.

Chronic illness and mental health representation are a few main themes in **Mistletoe Misconduct** and will be in each of my books in some way.

This is an open-door romance with lots of consensual spice. If you aren't a fan, this book may not be for you, or you're welcome to refer to the "Naughty List" on the following page so you know which chapters to avoid.

For a detailed list of events, please feel free to contact the author via Instagram DMs or email at Giuliana.Victoria.Author@gmail.com with any specific questions you may have about the contents of this book. While **Mistletoe Misconduct** is filled with lots of light and laughter, some themes may be triggering for people. Your mental health is always a priority. Never be afraid to ask for specific chapters

to avoid or to just avoid reading the book entirely.
Please take care of your mental health <3

The Naughty List

Playlist

Mistletoe — Justin Bieber
Christmas (Baby Please Come Home) — Mariah Carey
All I Want for Christmas Is You — Mariah Carey
Oh Santa! — Mariah Carey
Santa Tell Me — Ariana Grande
It's Beginning to Look a Lot like Christmas — Michael Bublé
Jingle Bells — Pentatonix feat. Lang Lang
Feliz Navidad — Pentatonix feat. La Santa Cecilia
Silent Night — Pentatonix feat. The King's Singers
Oh, It's Christmas! — Jordin Sparks
Home For The Holidays — Pentatonix
The Greatest Gift — Leroy Sanchez
Jingle Bells —Hilary Duff, Banda Musicale
Drummer Boy — Justin Bieber
A Nonsense Christmas — Sabrina Carpenter
Underneath the Tree — Kelly Clarkson
DJ Play A Christmas Song — Cher

8 Days of Christmas — Destiny's Child
the b*tch who stole christmas — Boys World
Be Your Santa Claus — Charles Jones
December — Ariana Grande
Secret Santa — Gwen Stefani
santa doesn't know you like i do — Sabrina Carpenter
Rudolph The Red-Nosed Reindeer — Gene Autry
Let It Go — Idina Menzel
Santa Baby — Eartha Kitt[1]

---

1. Mistletoe Misconduct Playlist

Signature Fragrances

Leonora Bardot:
Yves Saint Laurent Black Opium Eau de Parfum
&
Malakai Davis:
Valentino Uomo Eau de Parfum

Foreword

This is going to be a long preface, so please sit tight. Before you get started, I want to point out a few things here. While this is not my usual story, as in, it's got a shorter timeline and way fewer words (hence, novella), this is still very much a "me" kind of novel.

There is still mental health and chronic illness representation, even if it's not explored quite as much as in my other books. And my characters are still diverse and have had extensive sensitivity reading to ensure I'm publishing books with the most accurate representation of the people I write about as possible. I know this book (nor any books I write) is going to fulfill the need for BIPOC stories in romance because this is *not* a BIPOC story; it's merely a story with some BIPOC characters. I write diversity in my stories because I have the privilege of being surrounded by diversity in my personal life in all aspects, but also because, frankly, I think writing a book with an all-white cast or even with BIPOC as solely side characters feels fucking strange. BIPOC exist in the world, as they damn well should, so when I develop characters in my mind, I think up characters I find attractive, and sometimes I pick an ethnicity, culture, or race based on who is predominantly impacted in the real world by the mental health or chronic illness conditions I've chosen for the book. This is not to replace BIPOC stories written by actual BIPOC; it's not intended to, nor should it. I'll be including a list of BIPOC stories written by BIPOC authors who I adore at the end of this book—please check them out!

That said, I recognize that hockey is dominated by white males and that it may not be realistic to feature a Black MMC and an Arab female goalie, or even a gay head coach for a male team. Santa and Mrs. Claus probably aren't real either, but people still talk about them all the time. So enjoy this *very* fictional, *very* smutty little book, and I swear to Santa, if a single one of you reads this and *still* decides to email me your one-star review, I WILL blast you on social media (feel free to leave your one stars wherever you write reviews, just don't invade my personal space with them).

This is your one and only warning.

Also, I'd like to make myself clear when I say that sex work is *real* work. Those who partake in it should be paid for it, and those who enjoy partaking should be willing to pay for it. So when someone says someone else is a creep in this book, please don't take that as my personal opinion on those who enjoy consensual acts like those displayed in this work of *fiction*. Each character has to have their own personality and beliefs, and they certainly aren't all going to reflect my own. That would just be boring.

The absolute last disclaimer I will make is that you need to suspend SOME disbelief here. I considered having Kai wear long sleeves to cover his tattoos while on camera, but you know what? That's just not nearly as sexy as a tatted MMC, fully nude. So let's pretend he wouldn't be easily identifiable based on his tattoos, and that tiny lace masks actually would protect someone's identity. While we're at it, we're also going to pretend that the hockey aspects of this book (which are minimal) are also factual... It's a novella, not an encyclopedia, so enjoy it for what it is.

Now sit back, relax, and have yourself a very smutty holiday season.

This one's for anyone spending the holidays alone or away from your loved ones.
I hope you all have a very smutty little holiday season (for those who celebrate) <3
&
For Sarah from Hockey Smut Book Club. Stay cunty, bestie <3

Prologue: Lea

Friday, October 11, 2024

Sighing heavily, I tuck my tall frame behind what feels like the hundredth overgrown bush, holly berries threatening to poke my eye out. "Goddamnit, *hurry up*," I whine under my breath while waiting for Grant, my best friend's long-time boyfriend, to finally get down on one knee and propose. I've been following them along this trail for nearly an hour. The sun is setting, the bugs are swarming, and my ankles are itchy as shit.

My neck feels stiff, and I'm overheated despite the familiar New York autumn chill. If he doesn't hurry the hell up, I'm going to lose the golden hour glow, and *that* might piss me off even more than the giant rash I'm bound to be applying ointments and lotions to all week.

My heart leaps when I see him *finally* drop to his knee in the perfect location. The sun is setting in the background, and I have a perfect view of the small, secluded waterfall behind them to their right. It looks like something out of a movie, and god, I'm so damn excited for them.

Mona is busy pointing ahead, chatting enthusiastically about a plant that's in bloom today and how exciting it is getting to see it because it has to be at just the right time of day. Mona loves horticulture, and suddenly, I realize exactly why he waited until this moment. *Just the right time.*

"Mona," he calls to her when she still hasn't stopped talking long enough to realize he's no longer beside her.

Her long black waves swish across her back as she twirls to find where his voice came from.

Grant's lips part, and a soft expression crosses his face when she finally sees him down on one knee. I angle my camera toward them, immediately snapping photos, not wanting to miss a single second of this special moment. He sucks in a breath and starts speaking. "Mona Ayad..."

I capture the moment her hand smacks over her mouth in surprise. The moment she drops her hand and her whole face lights up with a brilliant smile. The moment she falls into his arms.

She grabs his cheeks in her hands, squeezing them together as she kisses him over and over, her response nothing but a garbled stream of consciousness.

My heart flies high as I take countless photos of one of the most life-changing events in my best friend's life.

Prologue: Kai

Friday, October 11, 2024

"**H**ey, I'll meet you back at home. Coach asked me to meet him in his office, and I don't wanna keep him waiting," Liam explains as he gathers up his gear.

"No problem. Hopefully, it's something good and not you getting your ass reamed out again," I joke.

He rolls his eyes up at me as he straightens. "Yeah, right. I think you're speaking about *yourself*. But whatever it is, I'm sure it's going to be fine."

He gives me a side hug before heading down the corridor to Coach's office.

My feet are propped up on the coffee table as I watch the New York Monsters play their first game of the hockey season. As usual, the only player worth a shit on that whole damn team is their goalie, Luca De Laurentiis.

I hear the familiar jingle of keys, and then the door unlocks as Liam pushes his way inside. The door gets stuck in the same place each time, and he has to ram it open with his shoulder.

I press mute on the remote before meeting his wide smile. "I take it things with Coach went well?"

He dumps his gear on the ground in the entryway and catapults toward me on the couch, landing beside me. Liam's hands grip my shoulders and shake me with excitement.

"You're gonna have to tell me what's going on before I wind up with whatever the adult version of shaken baby syndrome is," I tell him, laughing as he struggles to get his words out.

"I'm in! I'm fucking in, Kai!" he shouts with wide eyes. When he can't contain it any longer, he jumps up from the couch, performing an exaggerated version of his usual celly. I guess it may just *look* more exaggerated without all the pads.

I snort loudly. "Hey, man, I'm really happy for you, but I actually have no idea what the hell it is you're talking about, so could you sit your ass down and help a guy out?" I ask, still amused by his behavior.

Liam is usually the calm, cool, and collected one on the team. He never gets in trouble, never stays out late, and can always articulate his feelings. So whatever *this* is, it is not usual for him.

"I GOT DRAFTED! I'm gonna be a fucking Philly Scarlet!" he screams in my face.

I stand immediately, grabbing his shoulders because now it's *my* turn to shake the life out of *him.* "Holy shit!" I yell, grabbing him around the waist and swinging him around our living room like a rag doll.

My face feels hot, and my knees are weak. *He fucking did it!*

"This calls for celebration!" he says when I finally place him back on his feet, his cheeks red and his hair disheveled.

I couldn't agree more. My best friend is about to be living the dream, just like he deserves.

Chapter One

Lea

Saturday, November 30, 2024

It's the first time since high school that I've lived anywhere that wasn't with Mona, but I knew when Grant asked me to help with the proposal that the time would be coming soon.

It makes sense. Mona's nothing if not practical, and as much as she loves Grant, she would never marry someone without living with them first. She likes things a certain way, and they should find out sooner rather than later whether they're as compatible under the same roof as they are elsewhere.

Regardless of all that, I can still feel my heart thumping violently against my ribs as I make my way up to the third floor of Liam's apartment. Or at least what used to be his apartment.

Evidently, when Mona decided to move out, she also refused to let me figure it out on my own. I got a call from my brother the same night that she told me she was planning to move in with Grant. Liam said that Kai had been struggling to make rent since he left last month, and he was convinced that us moving in together would be the perfect solution.

I halt in my tracks, mere feet from the door, when I hear a familiar voice billowing through it.

"No, Liam! You know exactly why she can't fucking be here!" Kai all but screeches from the other side of the door.

My grip tightens on my luggage handle, and I can't help but shift on my feet, apprehension freely flowing through me. I knew this wouldn't be easy, but I hadn't realized Kai had *this* much of a problem with me.

"Kai, come on, man. You're being unreasonable. She's going to be here any second. Please don't let her hear you like this," Liam pleads quietly.

Too late.

I can't bring myself to interrupt, so here I stand, embarrassed, confused, and *annoyed.*

I could've found my own damn place. I definitely didn't need to move in with Kai, of all people, but *no.* Liam convinced me I'd be doing both of them a favor.

I guess this goes to show that was a fucking lie.

"No, Liam. I can't do this. You know I can't," he says. His last words sound small and defeated. It almost makes me feel bad for him.

Almost, but not quite. He's still an ass.

I hear whispered words between them, but I can't make out what they're saying.

Just as I'm about to raise my fist and knock, the door swings open, slamming against the wall behind it. Kai's dark eyes narrow as he takes me in, fists clenched at his side while he storms past me.

"Nice to see you too," I mumble sarcastically, rolling my luggage behind me.

Liam's brows shoot up his forehead when he sees me amble through the doorway. "Hey!" he shouts, his voice high-pitched, and he sounds a little too excited to see me.

He doesn't wait for me to respond or even put my things down before his arms wrap around me in a crushing hug.

"I've missed you!" he says, his voice sounding off.

He finally releases me, and I take a step back, letting go of my suitcase.

"Liam," I say, my voice acting as a warning that he's about to get his ass handed to him.

"Please, Lea. *Please*, don't start. I wasn't lying—he *does* need you to take my place. He can't afford it on his own. He's got a lot of personal shit going on with his mom that he wants to keep pretending isn't happening, but it is. He doesn't like talking about it, and you've known him your whole life. *You* know he never asks anyone for help." He grips the meaty part of my arms, his eyes pleading with me. "Just do this for me, okay?"

This motherfucker.

I groan loudly, unwilling to let him get off scot-free. "Liam, if he doesn't want me here, neither of us," I say, pointing between us, "can make the decision for him. He needs to be the one to decide this. For *himself*."

Liam hangs his head, rubbing the back of his neck as he releases a long sigh. "I hate it when you're right," he says with a groan. When he looks back up to meet my eyes, a pair of twin emeralds that mirror my own shine back at me with so much hope in them. "Just let me talk to him one more time before you leave, okay? Now that he's had some time to cool off, yeah?"

"Fine," I agree, dragging my luggage to Liam's old room. "But I've got to get to practice, and I'm not dragging my shit back downstairs beforehand, so he's just gonna have to deal with me taking up space in your old room for the day."

"I'll let you know what he ends up deciding before you get done at practice."

Mona and I sit beside each other on the locker room bench, drenched in sweat with our chests heaving.

My muscles are fatigued as hell, and I feel a twinge of a headache coming on. "You have an electrolyte packet in your bag?" I ask Mona, and she nods, bending forward to rifle around in her duffel. When she finds one, she tosses it to me.

"Thanks." I nod at her, pouring it into what's left of my water.

"I'll order another—" she says, her words getting cut off mid-thought. "Shit, I guess I *won't* order another box for the apartment."

My heart sinks just the smallest bit. "It's fine. I'll pick some up on my way back to Liam's."

She raises a dark brow at me as she stands to undress for a shower, now that we've caught our breath.

"And how's that going? Kai okay with you moving in?"

I roll my eyes at her. "No, apparently, Liam hadn't even asked him, so I had the immense displeasure of arriving to hear them bickering like an old married couple. I knew Kai was never my biggest fan, but I guess I never realized just how much he can't stand m e."

Her brows pinch together, confusion written plainly on her face. "Lea, I think you're delusional. That man looks at you like he wants to eat you for all three meals and snacks in between."

"Now who's the delusional one?" I ask, rolling my eyes as I get up to head to the showers.

"Clearly, still you. I'm sure there's a perfectly logical explanation for why he wouldn't want you living with him. Hell, maybe he doesn't think he'll be able to keep his hands off of you," she says, wiggling her eyebrows suggestively.

"Yeah, don't think that's it," I say with a laugh. Thankfully, our conversation is cut short as we enter our separate stalls by our teammate's voices that are too loud to speak over the partition.

By the time I make it back to my car, Liam's left me two voicemails and six texts. All of which tell me that Kai has "gotten over himself" and is "happy to have me." Which I'm certain are Liam's words, not Kai's.

I shake my head, toss my phone in the passenger seat, and head back to the apartment. I'll have to take Liam's word for it because, as it stands, I don't have anywhere else to go anyway.

Chapter Two
Kai

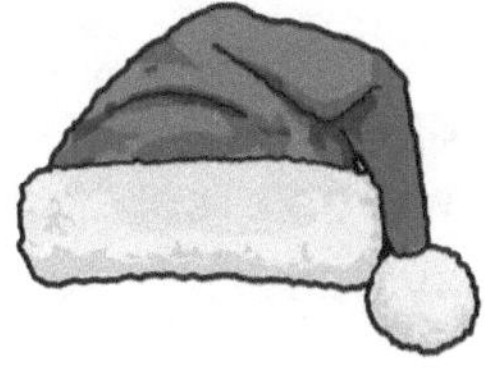

I can't believe that fucker got me to say yes.

Actually, scratch that, I *can* believe it. But that doesn't mean I like it.

The worst part is that Liam has a game tonight, so he had to go before Lea got back, which is bound to make this much more awkward.

I'm sprawled out on the couch, my head resting on my forearms as I try and fail to keep my eyes on the TV when Lea makes her way inside.

Her sweet vanilla scent permeates the room, making me feel dizzy. My teeth grind at the thought. I hate how she's always had that effect on me.

"Hey, Kai," she says noncommittally as she passes me in the living room and lets herself into the room that used to be Liam's.

"Leonora," I say, working to control the tone of my voice and giving her a curt nod.

I can practically feel the eye roll she's giving me right now. She hates it when I call her by her first name.

Which is precisely why I do it.

Yes, I realize I'm a grown-ass, twenty-six-year-old man, but it's the simple pleasures in life that make the world go round. And mine happens to be childishly calling my best friend's little sister a name she despises.

It's her fault though.

Maybe if she weren't so goddamn pretty, I wouldn't have to say dumb shit to keep her at arm's length.

Chapter Three

Lea

Sunday, December 1, 2024

My head is pounding when I wake up, and it feels like even the low hum of the city below could make my brain explode.

When music trickles from under the door, causing the nerves firing in my skull to match the beat of the loud song, I want to cry.

I want to fucking sob into the pillow because this shouldn't be my life, but it is.

No one should have to live like this.

And usually, I don't.

But the stress of the move, combined with the fact that I haven't been able to afford to pick up my prescription for BioNeur, is the perfect storm for a migraine from hell.

When the music only gets louder, I toss myself out of bed and practically crawl to the door. A swallow works in my throat as I twist the cold metal doorknob, opening the door a fraction. I peer out through the crack, careful not to let too much light in. "Kai," I call softly because even the sound of my own voice is like an ice pick through my ears.

When he doesn't hear me, I try again, now with watery eyes and an uncontrollable whimper leaving my throat. "Kai," I call out, hoping like hell he hears me this time.

I know he does when I see his back tense before he finally turns to face me. "Leonora," he greets me, his voice filled with disdain.

"Could you—" My voice wobbles. "Could you please turn it down?"

It takes every ounce of my strength to remain upright, as I hope like hell he agrees.

I watch as his brows pinch and his eyes narrow at me. He picks up the remote for the speaker, and hope swells in my chest.

But it's gone as quickly as it came, and the volume climbs.

Pain explodes in my skull, bringing me to my knees as I sob. I crawl back into my room, closing the door and locking it. I take small sips of water from the tumbler on my nightstand, hoping basic acetaminophen will do the job this time.

Except that I know it won't because it *never does.*

Nothing besides the BioNeur ever works, and without a generic on the market until the patent runs out in another eight years, I'm shit out of luck.

My crappy health insurance doesn't cover BioNeur, despite my migraines being refractory to every other drug on the market. But that's the thing. They aren't looking out for people; it's all about the money.

Once I've swallowed the pills, I feel around the bottom of my bag for my headphones, grab a blanket and pillows from the bed, and make my way to the closet. I set up a little nest for myself, hoping the cool, dark closet with minimal noise will ease the pain.

Relaxing into the pillows, I fight to calm the raging emotions and pain searing through me. I think the music has quieted, but that may be my imagination.

The same way that the knock on my door probably is too.

It's likely been hours that I've been lying here, which means Kai should be at practice. Luckily, we shouldn't have to see too much of one another because we have opposing hockey schedules since we play for the same organization, just on different teams.

I make my way out of the closet, grabbing my tripod and camera from the box in the corner of the closet before shutting the doors.

I flick on a lamp, hoping like hell it's enough light for what I need tonight. I can't handle more than this, and it already feels like it's too much.

Standing at the end of the bed, I stare at it, trying to decide what I need to do to make it presentable.

I start fluffing pillows as if they're actually going to be in the shot. Newsflash: *they aren't.*

But it's all about the vibes with this kind of work, so I do my best to make the bed look nice, opting to keep the fluffy white comforter on top.

When it's all fixed up, I grab my tumbler, filling it in the kitchen, and ensuring the coast is clear before locking my door and crawling onto the bed.

I work to make sure I've got the right angles before turning my laptop on and cueing up the chat room for *Mastur-chat.* "Shit," I curse, bounding off of the bed to grab my favorite pink vibe from the luggage I was too tired to unpack last night.

As soon as I'm in position, I turn the camera on and get to work.

Chapter Four

Kai

We got out of practice early because it was Coach's daughter's birthday, and apparently, he couldn't be an hour late or his husband would castrate him.

Good thing too because I'm beat.

I head into the apartment, dumping my gear in the hallway closet before making my way into the kitchen. My throat constricts. "Did I take my meds today?" I question for what may as well be the hundredth time today.

Opening the cabinet, I reach up to grab a glass, filling it with water from the fridge. My pills no longer sit in the same cabinet as the water cups because I have very little desire for Lea to find out about them.

Which is already posing a problem for me because I'm a creature of habit, and not having them in the same spot makes me feel like I didn't take them at all.

My cell pings, another chaotic message from my mom popping up on the screen. None of it makes any sense, but that's not unusual.

It only acts as yet another reminder that I need to stay on top of my pills. Otherwise, *I'll end up just like her.*

I grab the pills from their new place on my nightstand and dump them out on the kitchen counter, counting each one just to be sure.

A loud sound comes from Lea's room, and my head snaps in that direction.

"Yes, yes, yes," she moans out loudly.

My fist clenches at the thought of someone else being in there with her. *You have no right,* I try and fail to remind myself as I swipe the remaining pills into the bottle, recap it, and stomp over to her room.

She continues moaning loudly, so much so that it almost sounds... rehearsed?

Is she fucking with me?

"That's it, Candy Ass. Fuck that pretty pink pussy," an unfamiliar man encourages.

A chill runs down my spine from his voice. He sounds like a creep.

Suddenly, the low-level hum I hadn't even registered is cranked up, and I realize she must be playing with herself.

"Ooh," she cries, this time so much more believable than before. Her breath is coming in soft pants, and my dick is growing hard in my gym shorts. "Fuck, yes!" she screams.

My tongue darts out to wet my lip, and I feel my heart rate speeding up. I resist the urge to stroke myself right here, outside of her room.

Shit. Am I the creep?

"Oh, god..." She continues moaning. The vibrations get louder, changing pace as her metal bed frame knocks rhythmically against the wall.

The moment she meets her climax, I know it. She gasps softly, and the mattress beneath her groans as she settles back into it.

Moments later, she giggles softly. "Thank you for the tip, Fred. It's always a pleasure to serve you," she says, her voice holding a breathless, happy quality. "See you next time, everyone."

I hear her laptop shut, and I *know* I should move, but I can't seem to get my legs to work. I'm stuck here, about to get caught listening to whatever the fuck *that* was.

Chapter Five

Lea

T hank the lord for endorphins. That orgasm cleared up what was left of my migraine from earlier, and the tip Fred left me tonight was more than enough to cover the cost of a week of BioNeur. Hell, I could even get some *real* groceries this week.

"Talk about a Christmas miracle," I say, laughing to myself.

I toss on a pair of shorts and grab my tumbler, ready for a refill and a snack.

I open my door, and my hand flies to my chest. "Ah!" I screech, eyes wide as I take in the hulking figure standing mere inches from my door.

"What the fuck, Kai!" I shout at him, but instead of his usual retort, his jaw is hanging, and his eyes are as wide as saucers.

When he recovers, he snaps his mouth shut, only to open it again and start yelling at me. "What the fuck, me? How about what the fuck, you! Seriously Lea, does your fucking brother know you're making porn?!" he shouts at me, and the way his eyes bulge and judgment leeches into his tone has me hunching over, gripping my stomach as laughter bellows out o f me.

Who the hell does this man think he is? A loud snort leaves me before I can straighten and face the apparent wrath of Kai. Joke's on him, though. This is nothing new. I've dealt with his mood swings my whole life, and frankly, it's only made me want him more. Yes, he's an asshole, but something about how damn flustered he gets just makes me enjoy the chase. I think it's cute.

Kind of like a raccoon with rabies.

It'll tear your face off and ultimately end in your untimely demise, but people still call them trash pandas and try to keep them as house pets.

By the time I'm standing straight again, Kai's warm brown eyes are filled with confusion and annoyance.

"What the hell is so funny, Lea?" he asks, crossing his arms over his chest. The light from the kitchen casts shadows against his brown skin and makes his biceps look even more cut. *Damn him and his attractive everything.*

"You're overreacting," I tell him, pushing past him and making my way to the kitchen. "And it's not porn," I clarify.

"Well then, what the hell is it?" he asks, his voice sounding even more grumpy, and I just want to pinch his cheeks when he gets like this. *Annoying pain in my ass.*

"I'm a cam girl, Kai. In case you hadn't noticed from all the time you spent in *my* home growing up, my family isn't made of money, and the women's AHL team certainly isn't paying the big bucks."

"Why this though? Can't you do something else to make up the extra money?"

"Are you dense, or what?" I ask, hopping up on the cold granite counter. I know he can't stand it when I do this, which only makes me do it more often. "Do you really think I could play such a physically demanding sport, travel with my team, and hold down another conventional job? Seriously?" I ask, opening one of the dark wooden cabinets beside me and grabbing a pack of peanut butter crackers.

My brother's allergic to peanuts, so I know they're Kai's, and he only confirms that when he stomps over to me and snatches them out of my hand.

"These are *mine*," he grumbles.

A loud laugh bursts out of me, and when he gives me that inscrutable look of his, I suck my lips into my mouth, trying to hold in the laughter threatening to erupt out of me. I snake my hand inside the cabinet, grabbing another pack out and tearing into it, stuffing two crackers into my mouth.

Kai's eyes bulge, and suddenly, I'm reminded of just how much fun it was to pick on him growing up. In recent years, he's done a lot more of the tormenting, but with our current living arrangement, it seems the tables have turned yet again.

"I can barely afford to pay half of the rent on my old apartment, which is why I'm *here*. I don't make enough to feed myself, and I sure as shit don't have enough to pay for my meds—" His eyes widen ever so slightly on that word, but I keep speaking. "The only thing keeping a roof over my head, food in my stomach, gas in my tank, and my brain from exploding is this job," I tell him, sliding off the counter. "And the orgasms are nice, too," I say, leaving his stunned expression with an exaggerated wink.

Just when I think I've stunned him into silence, he's suddenly at my back, gripping my hips and spinning me to face him.

At five foot eleven, I meet his gaze, mere inches from mine, but if I were shorter, I'd have to crane my neck to look up at his six-foot-four height as he tries to tower over me.

"If you don't quit, I'm telling your brother," he tells me.

I rear back as if he'd smacked me, eyes wide with shock. "I don't know if you realize this or not, Kai, but I'm a fucking adult. As I already said, but don't worry, big guy," I say, patting his chest, "I'll repeat it for you since you seem to be having trouble understanding tonight and didn't get it through your thick skull." I cough dramatically into my fist. "Kind of like you couldn't manage to get the puck into the net the other day," I say, speaking out of one side of my mouth.

Watching the way his face twists with my words is going to bring me joy for a *long* time to come.

"As I was saying, my parents don't have any money, *Kai*. My brother is finally making decent enough pay to help not only himself but also them. And if you so much as mention me struggling to pay for a goddamn thing, let alone *how* I'm managing, he'll throw it all away for me. Liam will sleep in a fucking cardboard box to make sure I have what I need, and you know it. So if you love him the way you claim to, you'll keep your mouth shut and mind your own goddamn business," I finish, sucking in a much-needed deep breath.

His eyes narrow, but he takes a step back. "Fine." That's all he says before he stomps back to his room like a child who didn't get his way.

So, like the child I am sometimes, I call over to him. "Don't worry, Kai. There's more than enough room in my bed for you too. With those sexy goalie hands of yours? We could be loaded."

He glares over his shoulder at me and slams his bedroom door shut.

I chuckle lightly to myself, reaching into the cabinet for his jar of honey-roasted peanut butter and a spoon from the drawer below. I take the whole thing into my lair as if I'm a dragon protecting my most prized possession as my reward for managing to win my first battle with my new roomie.

Chapter Six

Kai

Monday, December 2, 2024

By the time my alarm goes off, I still haven't slept.

Frankly, I'm pissed about it. Schizophrenia is sensitive to changes in sleep cycle, and I have zero interest in doing a damn thing to perturb it.

And of course, it's all *her* fault.

Fucking Lea.

It was bad enough that I had those sexy fucking sounds that she made playing on repeat in my mind all night, but then she had to go and add fuel to the fire by inviting me into her bed. Whether or not she really meant the offer doesn't matter. It's the fact that there ever was any kind of offer that my brain kept snagging onto as I tried desperately to sleep.

But each time I'd close my eyes, I'd imagine what it'd be like if it were me in that room with her. If the camera were angled at nothing but her gorgeous pussy, or what I imagine it would look like anyway. I picture how well she'd take my fingers, screaming my name instead of praising someone else's sky daddy.

I clutch the sides of my head, clenching my eyes shut and willing the images of her to stop.

"Fuck!" I shout, climbing out of bed and snagging a pair of shorts before slipping into my sneakers and going for a run.

By the time I get back, I'm exhausted and grateful as hell that I don't have practice or a game today. I need this day just to relax and get back on track.

I gulp down a glass of water and take a much-needed shower, but when I get out, my phone is ringing from where I'd left it on the kitchen counter.

Shit.

I wrap a towel around my waist, running into the other room, and answer just in time.

"It's Kai," I rush out, my breath coming out in pants, much like it does every time I get a call. More often than not, when someone's calling me, it's Mom. And she always needs something.

"Kai, baby," she coos on her end of the line, and my heart splits in two. Not *again.*

"I need you to come pick me up, baby." She lowers her voice to a whisper. "They found out, Kai. They found out, and I need you to come get me out of here."

"Found out about what, Mom?" I ask, trying not to sound as exasperated as I feel.

"About the messages, baby. They found out, and just like I told you, they want to do tests on me, but you can't let them!" she starts shouting, becoming hysterical.

"Mom. Mom," I plead, trying to draw her attention back to me. "You've gotta be quiet, or they'll hear you talking about it and I won't be able to get you out, okay?"

"Okay," she whispers back.

A heavy sigh leaves my lips at her acceptance. It's not always this easy. Hell, *usually* it isn't easy at all. When she stops taking her meds and gets like this, it can seem impossible to bring her back.

"Tell me where you are, and I'll come get you. Don't worry, I won't let anyone do any tests on you, alright?" I try to keep my voice as even as possible, but anxiety is threatening to strangle me.

"Ma'am, may I speak with your son?" A man's deep voice travels over the line, and Mom starts shouting at him to get back.

There's a commotion, and I realize exactly where she's at by sound alone.

"I'll be there soon, officer," I say loud enough that I hope he can hear me despite their attempts to restrain my mother.

Again.

If I thought I was exhausted before, I was wrong.

When I get inside, I toss my keys down on the kitchen counter, and they land with a loud thud.

Lea's lying on the couch with a fuzzy pink blanket draped over her legs as she watches game tape.

"Hey." She waves at me, but I don't have the energy to speak, so I just nod, heading back to my room.

I collapse on the bed, closing my eyes and hoping like hell that when I wake up from this day, it'll all just have been a nightmare.

Unfortunately, that's not my reality.

What is though? My mother forgetting her meds enough times that she landed herself in jail. Again.

And of course she can't hold down a job long enough to be able to afford her bail. So here I am, the proud new owner of a massive fucking loan and a newly drained savings account.

It'll be fine, I try to tell myself. *I can just get another job. Some little side gig.*

But the longer I lay here sorting through what that would entail, the more I realize what a fucking dick I'd been to Lea last night.

Goddamnit.

My eyes snap open as I have an epiphany, seemingly from hell.

I should call the big guy downstairs and ask him to prepare my rotisserie spit because when Liam finds out about this, I'll be meeting him sooner than either of us had planned for. I drag my ass over to the living room, forcing myself to look Lea in the eyes as she peers up at me.

"If your offer still stands, I'm in," I tell her.

I watch as her white brows twist in confusion, those pink lips of hers pinching as she processes my words. "What offer?" she finally asks. Apparently, she's more forgetful than I'd thought.

"Money, goalie hands, camera, creepy dudes," I huff out, swinging my arms around as I explain.

She stares blankly at me, and the moment she gets it, I know because her expression changes from confusion to shock.

"Oh my god, seriously, Kai? That was *not* a real offer!" she shouts at me.

"It sure as shit sounded like one!" I shout back at her.

"Well," she says, blowing out an exasperated breath. "It wasn't." She rolls her pretty green eyes at me just the way I like, and that thought alone should have me taking her denial for the blessing it is. But instead, I plant my ass beside her and get to begging.

"What if it *was* an offer though, Lea? Think about it; you were right." Her brows shoot up to her hairline at that admission, so I trudge on, hoping to avoid admitting that again. "We could make a fuck ton of money, and it wouldn't even have to be you doing the work. We could set rules, *boundaries*," I emphasize. "I could use just my hands to get you off or even just your toys."

Suspicion is evident in her tone. "Why the sudden change in tune?"

"I've had"—I clear my throat—"a change in financial situation that warrants an additional source of income."

"Uh huh, and this change happened between last night and right now?"

I groan, dropping my head into my hands as I mumble, "Unfortunately, yes."

"Fine."

My head snaps up, and I balk at her. "Fine?"

She nods. "Yep. Fine. Only your hands and my vibes. Don't show your face so you don't end up in the news, and I'm not doing any of the fucking work," she tells me as she stands, heading to her room. "And Kai?" she asks, looking over her shoulder at me as I remain seated and stunned.

"Yeah?"

"This is on a trial basis. If your meaty hands drive down my viewership, you're on your own."

Of course I am.

That's how it usually feels.

Chapter Seven

Lea

Friday, December 6, 2024

"And you just, what? Offered to let him join your *solo* party?" Mona asks, her hands on her hips as she stares down her nose at me.

"Sort of, yeah." I shrug. "It started as a joke to ruffle his feathers a bit, but then when he asked about the next day, he seemed sort of desperate, and dollar signs flashed in my mind, so I kind of just went with it."

"Okay…" she says, blowing out a breath and taking a seat beside me on the frozen bench outside of the rink. "You know not to get attached, right? Because I know you've had a crush on him since we could walk, but this will mean *nothing* to him. You've gotta promise me you'll remember that."

I wave a hand in the air dismissively. "I know, I know. Don't worry. It'll just be a few awkward orgasms, and my views will probably tank and that'll be that."

"Why would they tank?" she asks, her dark brow raised questioningly.

"Because my viewers don't like to share, so I can't imagine they'd be all that interested in seeing another man get me off."

She nods slowly, understanding dawning. "Alright," she says, standing. "I guess let me know how it goes. I've gotta get home for date night, but I'll see you tomorrow for our game."

"I'll keep you posted," I say, heading to my car.

As I sit on the edge of the bed, waiting for Kai to get home, my stomach is swarming with butterflies. I'm so damn nervous that I could puke.

And he's right—what if my brother finds out somehow? Then we're both screwed. He'd lose his fucking mind, and I'm not sure which part would be worse. The fact that I'm a cam girl or that Kai is joining me.

The sound of the door unlocking has me jumping a foot off the mattress.

"Fuck, I don't think I can do this," I whisper to myself.

I hear the telltale sign of him dumping his bag in the closet before he pops his head into my room.

"Leonora." He nods at me, a confident smirk plastered on his face.

"Hey," I squeak out, nerves getting the better of me. His expression changes as his lips smooth into a worried line.

"What's wrong?"

"Maybe this isn't such a good idea," I tell him, picking at my cuticles as I refuse to make eye contact.

He invades my space as if it's his own, taking a seat beside me on my bed. The mattress compresses under his weight, and my leg starts to bounce with anxiety.

Kai's warm hand presses down on my thigh, just above the knee, stopping the erratic movement of my leg.

"It's gonna be fine, Lea," he assures me.

Lea. Not Leonora. Just, *Lea.*

"I know you hate me, but I guarantee you won't have to fake an orgasm with me, and who knows, maybe your viewers will love it."

Oh, you sweet summer child. I could never hate him, but he doesn't need to know that.

"Alright, but I was serious. If my bank account is affected by this, you're out."

He nods in agreement. "Got it. I'm gonna go take a shower. I'll be ready in twenty. That enough time?"

"Yep," is all I manage to say.

I might have a heart attack in the next twenty minutes, and then we wouldn't have to do this at all. Though I'm pretty sure I wouldn't be able to afford whatever the hospital bill for *that* kind of workup would be.

Besides, Kai may be an ass, but he'd never hurt me, and half the time, I'm pretending my hand is his anyway.

Chapter Eight
Kai

F rigid water runs down my body, and a shiver wracks through me.

If I'm going to keep up this act and make Lea believe I'm really unaffected by her, I need all the help I can get. Frankly, I should start worrying about the water bill a bit more because I see a lot of ice-cold showers in my future.

By the time I make it out of the shower and make it over to Lea's room, she's already got everything set up.

When she peers up to meet my gaze, she seems a lot calmer than when I first got home.

"Hey, perfect timing," she says, beaming at me. "Before we get started, we need to double-check that you're gonna have enough room to keep your face out of the shot without accidentally knocking

anything over. So would you mind testing it out for m
e?"

I cough into my fist, clearing my throat before I
can even try to answer. "Yeah, uh, no problem."

It is very much a problem.

I position myself at the end of the bed, dodging
the tripod she has the camera set up on, and she
scoots to the very end, opening the screen on her
laptop to a full-screen view of what the camera is
about to be focused on. When she scoots her ass to
the end of the bed, angling her center at the camera,
what she does next nearly stops my goddamn heart.

She extends her long, toned legs into the air before dropping them to either side of the bed in a full
split.

"Jesus fucking Christ," I choke out. Her eyes glint
with mischief, and the little smirk she's wearing
goes straight to my cock.

So much for that cold shower.

"Like what you see?" she muses.

My breath gets lodged, and this time, I manage to
choke down the cough threatening to give me away.
I have the next hour to convince *both* of us that this
is just a business exchange, but when she leans back
on her elbows, pushing her perky little tits out, I
know I'm a goner.

I'll be thinking about this for the rest of my goddamn life.

Leonora Bardot is about to ruin me for every
woman I'll ever be with, and I haven't even seen all
of her yet.

Chapter Nine

Lea

T his is the easy part.

I'm able to dissociate enough that none of this bothers me because it's what I'm used to doing before every one of these live streams. Kai, on the other hand, now seems as bent out of shape as I had been when he first got home, but if the raging boner he's sporting is any indication, I think he'll be *just fine.*

When his hand hovers over me, I gaze at the laptop, ensuring the angle is exactly where it needs to be.

"That should be good, but make sure you can move around comfortably," I tell him and hear him grunt a reply. I pat the bed beside me, and he quirks a questioning brow at me. I roll my eyes. "Do you seriously intend to just stand at the end of the bed for the next hour?"

He huffs out a breath, clenching his eyes shut before crawling into bed beside me. His face stays out of focus, thanks to his height.

He hovers his hand back over my center, staring at the screen of my laptop, and his finger grazes my covered slit. He curses under his breath. "Shit, sorry," he says, pulling his hand away.

I muffle a laugh with the inside of my elbow before meeting his eyes. I reach out for his hand and lie it flat against me. His sharp inhale and the way he sucks his full bottom lip between his teeth already has my core clenching with need.

"You're literally about to have these fingers stuffed inside me. I think a little graze of your pinky is the least of our worries," I tell him, trying to keep the mood light, but judging by the way his eyes darken, it has the opposite effect. As if by speaking the words, they somehow just became *very fucking real.*

I pluck his hand off of me before scooting back on the bed so I can shimmy out of my clothes.

"Kai, are you ready?"

He nods, his expression still stuck somewhere between lust and anger.

"Use your words, Kai. Otherwise, we aren't doing this. And that's okay too. You can walk away from this unscathed. Just like I'm consenting to being watched by these men, and sometimes women, playing into their fantasies, you need to as well. Most of you won't be seen, but what we're about to do is intimate, and that means you've gotta consent."

"I want this," he says, blowing out a breath and running his hand over his dark, low-cut curls. He clears his throat the way he always does when he's about to lie to me. "I mean, I *need* this. Need the money."

He blows out another long breath, standing up from the bed. "Okay, if you want to stop at any point, just say so and this ends. I'll slam the laptop shut and be done with it. Okay?"

"Got it," he confirms, shaking out his arms and doing a little jog in place as if he's about to go for a run.

It makes me giggle as I toss my white crop top to the ground and slide my shorts off, positioning myself for the camera the same way I had been before.

"We'll start with panties on so you can work up to fingering me."

His eyes haven't left my lace-covered pussy in over thirty seconds, and I think I see some drool. "Just follow my lead," I tell him, turning the livestream on.

"Hello, my little kittens. It's Friday, which means I have a *very* special surprise for you today," I purr, using the most seductive voice I can manage. I feel a little silly putting on an act like this with Kai in the room.

I can already feel my skin burning up under his gaze.

"Someone will be joining us today. Someone with big, *strong* hands and a cock I want to choke on. Who knows? Maybe one day I will for you guys."

I smirk when I see all of the comments flooding through, so I prioritize the ones from people who send tips with their replies.

"I'm sorry, Jerry, there won't be any audio on your end today. As much as your sexy voice turns me on,"—I see Kai stiffen but ignore it—"I wouldn't want to distract our guest."

I read a few more, snaking my hand down to cup myself, gently circling my clit with my middle finger. "Okay, last question before I introduce him. Fred asked if we're together because he's afraid it'll break the fantasy for him. No, Fred, don't worry, he's just a visitor, nothing more."

That's a dead-ass lie, much like everything else I do in these chat rooms. I very rarely have a real orgasm on here. It's all too scripted, and it usually doesn't feel right.

I meet Kai's warm brown eyes, extending my hand for him to take so I can place it on me, just like I had earlier.

We maintain eye contact the whole time I'm speaking, and the bed sags beneath me as he crawls back into position, lying next to me. "This is our special guest; he's going to use his hands to fuck my sweet little cunt just the way I know he's been dreaming about."

A smirk crosses his lips, and it sets me at ease. He's *finally starting to relax into this and regain some of his playboy energy.*

I lean back onto the pillows, releasing Kai's wrist, and shoot him a wink, hoping he knows that means it's his time to take over.

When I start to get bored, I'll just fake an orgasm and resume my plans to rot on the couch for the rest of the night.

Except when Kai starts to take over, I know right away that we won't be able to go back to the way things were before.

His eyes never leave mine as he starts to swirl a finger over the lacy fabric before hooking it under the material and snapping it against my skin. It stings for a moment, but electricity crackles through my core at the contact.

"You like that, angel?" he asks, tugging the fabric to the side and running a fingertip through my slit.

I nod, my lips wobbling as I fight to remain as composed as possible.

"Don't go quiet on me now." He tsks. "Where's that loud mouth of yours? I think your viewers want to get what they paid for, yeah? So I wanna hear you fucking *scream*."

He slides his index finger in, pumping it and stretching me the slightest bit as my eyes practically roll to the back of my head.

"Can you do that, angel? Can you get nice and loud for us?"

"Yes," I pant, my chest heaving. I snake a hand up my abdomen, and when I find my nipple, I roll it between my thumb and forefinger. "God, yes." I moan when he positions his hand with his palm up so his thumb grazes my clit, and his other fingers apply the most glorious pressure to the sides of my pussy lips.

"You like that, don't you?"

"Uh-huh," I cry out. My hands shoot to my sides, gripping the sheets as he repositions his hand so his middle and ring fingers are inside of me.

I finally break eye contact so I can stare at the screen, watching how he fucks me. He twists his wrist so his palm is down and spreads his fingers inside me. A loud groan claws up my throat.

"Fuck, yes, give me more," I moan, begging for anything he'll let me have.

The mattress dips under his weight again as he slides himself behind me. My knees drop to either side, opening myself wide for him, and I feel his warm chest pressed against my cool, sweat-sheened back.

His arms wind around me, and a second hand joins. He pinches my clit, alternating between pinching and applying firm pressure.

"When all the cameras are away, what do you plan to do with me tonight?" he asks, his voice rough, and heat sears through me. My back arches as he adds another finger, increasing his pace.

"I—" I can't answer because there won't be anything after this.

"Come on, angel. This is show-and-tell, baby. I'm showing, you're telling. So tell everyone how you plan to choke on my dick later."

I pry my eyes from the screen to look up at him. He's watching me with rapt attention, and when his brow quirks in challenge, I give in as I ride his hand, silently pleading for *more*.

"When the cameras are off," I start, panting, "I'll get on my knees for you and play with my pussy while you choke me. I want your hands in my hair, pulling at my roots as I slobber all over your thick cock."

"That's more like it, angel. Now, scream for Daddy," he says, maintaining his smirk as he spreads his fingers inside me, pinching my clit again and quickly removing all contact. My eyes widen at the loss of sensation, and when his hand rears back, smacking my pussy with full force, I practically catapult off the bed. "Fuck!" I shout, and his fingers slam back inside me, pumping relentlessly. My skin feels raw and overly sensitive as if every nerve ending in my body is lighting up at the same time.

He swaps back to using just one hand, his palm slapping against my clit each time he plunges inside me. "Yes, just like that!" I scream, my legs squirming as I fight to stay in frame. "Please, keep going. Don't stop!"

Kai chuckles darkly. "While your juices are dripping down your pussy like this? For me? No, angel. This is a fucking dream come true. Now do the splits for me, baby, and let me see every inch of you come around my fingers."

My core clenches; jolts of pleasure buzz through me at his words and his touch.

"Give me everything, angel. I wanna see this gorgeous pussy come all over my hand."

His words are like a command to my body, and just like that, I'm vibrating off the bed. My walls clench tightly around his fingers, acting like a vice to hold him inside me. "Yes, yes! Oh fuck! Yes! That's—" I pant, my mind and body short-circuiting. "Oh *god.*" I groan. "That's incredible."

I slump against him, my limbs suddenly feeling boneless.

Chapter Ten

Kai

A small, sated smile sits prettily on Lea's puffy lips, swollen from biting on them while she whimpered so sweetly for me. I want to kiss that smile right off her face, devour her lips, and have h er *really* begging to fuck my dick with her throat, and not just for some creepy fucks on the internet.

Jealousy threatens to consume me at the thought that other people have seen her like this. Seen her delicious pussy spread out like a goddamn buffet. What none of them realize yet, Lea included, is that her pussy is now *mine*.

I reposition myself to sit beside her. I maintain eye contact with her, staring right into her glossy emerald eyes as I bring my fingers to my mouth and suck her right off of them.

The taste is sweet, a little salty, and all *Lea*.

God, I am so fucked.

Her breath hitches as she watches me, pupils dilating. She collapses back onto the pillows, swinging an arm over her eyes as she releases a loud groan followed by, "Fucking hell. We are so *screwed.*"

Yes, *sweet Lea, you're absolutely about to be screwed.*

And no one gets to watch but us.

She finally uncovers her face, looking over at the laptop with wide eyes as they flick across the screen.

"They—" she stammers. "They loved it! They love you!" Her giggle pings through the room, and a broad smile spreads my cheeks.

"Fuck yeah!" I shout, excited that I get the opportunity to do this again and hoping like hell that comments equate to cold, hard cash.

"Well, that's all for tonight, guys. As you can see, our guest here has a bit of a mess to clean up, but maybe if you're all good and send him lots of love and tips, he'll agree to come back again. Goodnight," she tells them, making a kissing sound before logging off.

She falls back onto the bed, kicking her arms and legs in the cutest, excited little dance I've ever seen.

"That was amazing!" she tells me, smiling brightly. "I mean, like, the comments. I'm glad they liked it!" she says, trying to conceal her true meaning.

I'm not sure what does me in. The fact that my dick is so hard right now I think a gentle breeze could make me blow, or the light-pink flush on her cheeks that contrasts with her platinum waves spread out across her pillows.

Whatever it is, I climb off of the bed, turn the camera off, set it aside, and drop to my knees at the end of the bed.

Her breath hitches as I grip her creamy thighs in my hands, dragging her ass to the edge of the bed and tossing her legs over my shoulders.

"Kai," she whispers. "I didn't really mean you had to clean me up."

"I know you didn't, but I want to. My momma always taught me that when I make a mess, it's my responsibility to clean it up," I tell her with a wry grin.

She told me no such thing. The woman can't even manage to clean up her own goddamn messes, let alone teach a child to do so, but Lea doesn't need to know that.

She sucks that pouty lower lip into her mouth as she sits up, balancing on her hands behind her so she can watch my every move.

I run my nose along her seam, coating my face in her wetness, and as it drips into my mouth, I lick it off before diving back in for more.

I use my fingers to spread her pussy lips wide, flicking my tongue over her clit and then diving in for a taste. Lea's tight pussy spasms around my tongue, and one of her hands scrapes over my head, holding my mouth to her.

I chuckle and love the way her body responds to the vibration of it.

My dick is begging to be let loose, so I reach down, tugging myself free of my gray sweats, and palm my shaft.

I slurp and suck on her pussy, maintaining the same rhythm as my hand on my dick.

"Kai, *please*, I'm about to come again," she cries.

"Damn right you are," I grunt out, licking a long stroke from her tight ass to her clit. "Come with me, baby. Pretend it's my dick inside you."

"It could be," she moans, and my eyebrows shoot up my forehead. There's no chance in heaven or hell that I heard her right. "Fill me up, Kai," she all but begs. "I want you buried inside me when you come, *please*."

I refrain from reminding her that her brother is going to castrate me, and instead, opt to just ignore her. I increase my pace on her clit, taking everything she can give me, and when her thick, muscular thighs clench the sides of my head, we come apart together.

"God, yes!" she shouts. My dick spurts all over the side of her bed, heat searing through me as my balls tighten, releasing every last drop.

When her breathing's returned to some semblance of normalcy, I lean back onto my heels, inspecting my handy work. "It appears I did a fabulous job with the cleanup. I got every last damn drop," I say with a wink before finally standing.

Her eyes widen, catching on my length, and I realize she's never seen it before.

"I've seen yours, so I guess it's only fair that you see mine," I tell her, chuckling deeply.

She sits up, swinging her legs off the side of the bed and reaching out for me. "Can I?" she asks, her wide eyes pleading.

I give her a nod, and she grips me in her palm, squeezing me tightly. And just like that, I'm hard again.

"Now I get why you didn't want to fuck me. You'd have torn me in two," she says.

Good fucking lord, woman. How goddamn wrong she is about my intentions. But I won't be admitting that.

This was a fucking mistake. I'm going to lose my best friend if we go any further than this, so as it stands, this is a business arrangement and nothing more.

But I'll definitely still be adding this to the top of my spank bank.

"Yeah, exactly," I tell her. "And, uh, we probably shouldn't do any of the off-camera stuff again. I haven't slept with anyone in a while and got a little carried away. Sorry about that."

If she's offended or upset, I can't tell because she just smiles up at me. "Yeah, you're right. Hopefully, we wake up to a fuck ton of cash," she jokes.

"Yeah," I say, scratching the back of my neck. "Well, enjoy the rest of your night," I tell her, backing out of her room so I can go screw my head back on straight in the comfort of my own room.

Chapter Eleven

Lea

Saturday, December 7, 2024

Just like I was afraid, things went from super hot to super not the moment the post-orgasmic endorphins wore off.

Kai disappeared into his room for the remainder of the night, and I didn't so much as see him grab a glass of water before I finally went to bed.

I roll over onto my side, grabbing my laptop from the nightstand, and logging into my Mastur-chat account.

The payment tab has a big red bubble over it that reads, *Five thousand, seven hundred thirty-two.*

Jesus Christ, that's a lot of people tipping!

When I click on it, I have an out-of-body experience. It's like the Ghost of Christmas Past is standing at the end of my bed, looking over my stunned, lifeless body.

I don't care how fucking awkward Kai is being, he'd want to know about this.

I toss my covers off, leaving my laptop on the bed as I sprint across the dark linoleum. I bang on Kai's door, and he grunts on the other side. "Let me in, or I'm letting myself in!" I call to him through the thin, white-painted wood panel.

"Go away," he groans out.

"Nope, coming in!" I shout, turning the knob, and to my delighted surprise, it's not locked.

I barge in, catapulting myself onto his bed. I'm straddling his waist, my fingers digging into his shoulders as I bounce with excitement.

Apparently, I'm not the only one who's excited here, though. Kai's morning wood rubs against my core, halting my movements. His hands clamp down on my hips, and he grits his teeth. "Quit moving, or I'm going to break my promise to stay away from you, and I'll be breaking something else instead," he rumbles beneath me.

Swinging my leg over so I can flop down on his bed, supporting my head with my forearms, I smile up at the ceiling. "Kai," I whisper.

"What is it, angel?" he asks, and my heart all but stops beating at the nickname. One he's never spoken until last night.

I push down the arousal threatening to take hold of me and roll onto my side to face him. "Your magical hands broke my viewers," I tell him. He stares at me blankly, clearly unsure of what I mean. "We got just shy of six thousand dollars in tips last night," I tell him, bursting with excitement.

He bolts upright, and his black satin bed sheet pools around his waist, revealing the most spectacular set of abs. The sunlight peeking through his blinds illuminates his smooth brown skin, and my eyes are seemingly stuck on him.

His gravelly, sleep-laden voice drags my attention back to his face. "Six *thousand?*"

I nod enthusiastically. "Yep! That's like"—I pause, doing the mental math—"two months and a week's worth of my medication," I tell him excitedly.

His brows pinch together, and all the air leaves my lungs.

Fuck.

"I ignored it the other day because it seemed like we had bigger fish to fry, but now that you're in my bed, you're gonna do as I say and tell me what the hell your meds are for."

I move to slide out of the bed, but his muscular arms wrap around my waist, hauling me backward until I'm flush against his chest.

"Tell me what the hell is going on, Lea," he grinds out, his lips brushing against my ear with each word, sending a chill down my spine.

"It's not that serious, Kai. I just don't like people in my business. I'm sure *you* can relate," I say, my voice dripping with sarcasm.

"If it's not that big of a deal, just tell me so I can get some goddamn rest."

"Aww, is little Kai staying up all night worrying about me?" I ask, fluttering my lashes at him as I twist in his arms to face him. That was a big mistake though. The change in position just brought my lips an inch from his, and suddenly it feels like all the oxygen in the room has been sucked out through a straw.

"You're well aware there's nothing little about me, Leonora. But go on with your poor attempts at deflecting," he says, chuckling.

I roll my eyes but decide just to tell him so I can get out of his arms and back to the safety of my own personal space.

"I have chronic migraines, and they're downright debilitating."

"Don't you have health insurance? You're required to by your team," he says as if I'm not already aware.

"I do, but my migraines are refractory to all other medications I've tried. Lifestyle changes haven't helped, and the only thing that consistently works is BioNeur, which isn't covered under my formulary and there isn't a generic. It's almost twenty-seven hundred a month," I explain, groaning as I wiggle out of his arms.

"Shit, I'm sorry, Lea. I hadn't realized."

I wave him off, not wanting nor needing his pity. "It's fine, Kai. We all have shit, and based on your sudden change in attitude, you're not exempt from that."

"You're right, I'm not." He sighs, lying back on the bed. "But this helps, so thanks for letting me take part."

I smirk down at him, pinching his stubbled chin between my forefinger and thumb. "The pleasure was all mine," I say with a wink, and when I move to take my hand back, he grabs my wrist, pulling me on top of him.

Kai's massive body rolls over me as we trade positions, with me on the bottom now.

I have to clench my thighs, need pulsing through me as he looks down at me. "I'd say it was pretty equal," he huffs, and I feel his warm breath coast over my lips. He lowers his head as he snakes his hand down my abdomen toward the apex of my thighs. "I bet you thought about it all night," he whispers, and he's not wrong.

I nod, agreeing because there's no use in denying it. I've wanted Kai my whole life. Now that I have him, I'm more than happy to take every ounce of him until he's no longer willing to give it.

His fingers work between my thighs, pushing them apart. He toys with a small silk bow on the waistband of my sleep shorts, and finally, he slips his hand inside, cupping me.

A soft moan leaves my lips, and I arch off the bed, wrapping my arms around his neck to bring him impossibly close to me.

"This is just practice," he whispers.

"For—" My voice wobbles. "For what?" I ask, my mind scrubbed clean of all responsibility and self-preservation.

"For our big show, angel. We need to get you those meds, and I've got some bills to pay. Practice makes perfect, so spread these pretty thighs and let me get my fill before you have to leave to catch your bus for the game tonight," he says, his voice husky and full of need.

My body responds of its own accord. I'm unsure I could will it to disobey, even if I wanted to.

He's sliding his finger through my folds, not penetrating yet, but I'm already soaked. I pout at him while he continues teasing me, and when my body is thoroughly on fire and I can't take anymore, I whine, "Kai, you're gonna have to give me more than that."

"How much more?" he purrs, his voice so goddamn sexy I could come from that alone.

"Everything," I moan.

He presses the pad of his thumb to my clit, lowering his lips to my ear. Goosebumps erupt over my arms as his lips tickle the shell of my ear.

"I don't think you can handle *everything*," he taunts. "But I'm willing to let you try." His pace speeds up, and he finally pushes his finger inside me, eliciting a loud, needy moan from me. My core clamps down around him, and I have to squeeze my eyes shut to recenter myself.

"You feel so good like this. So obedient as you take whatever I'm willing to give you," he says. "Now if you want my dick buried inside this tight, wet pussy, you're gonna fucking *beg*—"

His words are cut off by a sharp sound ringing out in the room. We shoot up in bed, looking around the room until our eyes land on his cell sitting on the nightstand. Kai scrambles off me, removing his finger and grabbing his phone. He answers the call without checking the screen, and the moment the phone is to his ear, he shoves his finger in my mouth. "Suck," he commands, pressing the phone to his chest for a brief second to muffle the word.

I suck myself off of his finger, and when he's satisfied, he pulls it from my mouth.

"Yeah, *Liam*. We're doing great. Everything's good here. Yeah, I'm sure a visit would be awesome," he says.

My heart starts hammering in my chest at the mention of my brother's name. God, this was a stupid fucking idea and Liam only acts as a reminder of that. I practically toss myself out of his bed, giving him an awkward wave before bounding out of there.

My eyes snag on a pill bottle on the top of his nightstand, but I don't linger long enough to figure out what it is, not that it's any of my business.

I wonder if his meds cost as much as mine and maybe that's why he needs the money like I do. *I think he would've told me that if it were the case though.*

I shake the thought away and trudge back to my room to start getting ready for my game tonight.

Chapter Twelve

Kai

Thursday, December 12, 2024

I won't deny that I've been avoiding Lea all week, and frankly, it's for her own good. Because one taste of her has driven me absolutely wild, and I want nothing more than to devour her pussy all day, every day.

Then, between our games and practices, it was easier to stay the hell away from her. And as much as I'd like to say I regret what we did, I can't. It felt too good, too natural, *too fun.*

Not to mention, when that three thousand dollars hit my bank account on Monday, a massive weight started to lift off my chest.

Now that we're both home, my heart rate is alarmingly high at the notion of being here with her *all night.*

We briefly spoke about doing another live tomorrow, so there's no reason for me to get this worked up over seeing her *tonight.*

I hear her at the door and frantically work to look relaxed, leaning back against the couch cushions and resting my head on my arm. "God, I look like a douche," I groan quietly to myself.

She pushes the door open, her eyes widening and mouth popping open to make the cutest little "o" shape when she sees me.

She recovers quickly though, flashing me a smile. "Hey, I hadn't expected you home."

"It's just a regular Thursday night, *Leonora,*" I say, rolling my eyes. "Of course I'm home."

Her fair cheeks turn a pretty rose color, and she bites that plump bottom lip, shifting her weight as she leans across the kitchen counter. Lea's wearing a pair of black spandex shorts and a red sports bra. All the skin she's showing is distracting as hell.

I clear my throat, my eyes flicking to the TV. "Wanna watch a movie or something?"

She scrunches her nose like a bunny, and a cute little line sits on the bridge of her nose. "Really?"

I adjust, letting my arm fall to my side before fixing my eyes on her. The confidence I'd felt moments before is suddenly sucked out of me. She reaches behind her head, causing her cleavage to practically overflow out of her top, and when she undoes her ponytail, I know I'm a goner.

Her platinum waves tumble down, cascading over her shoulders and framing her oval face.

Even just after a nearly two-hour-long practice, one I'm sure was brutal as the holidays approach and our coaches are trying to combat the excessive eating and drinking players tend to do, she's fucking devastating to look at.

Beautiful couldn't even begin to cut it.

"Kai?" she asks, her voice soft as she says my name.

"Yeah?" I ask, tilting my head.

She shakes hers, those waves flying around her face, and she breaks out in a small smile. "Put on Christmas Chronicles and I'll make popcorn," she tells me, heading over to the pantry.

"Yes, ma'am," I say, chuckling. I kind of like it when she orders me around.

Our tiny apartment smells like butter and salt as Lea plants herself on the cushion beside me. Being that this apartment is so damn small, Liam and I could only fit a loveseat in here, so there isn't a whole lot of space between us.

I glue my attention to the screen. "You ready to start?" I ask.

"Mhmm," she mumbles, grabbing the blanket hanging over the back of the couch. "Hold this," she says, shoving the bowl of popcorn in my hands.

Lea scoots around, fixing the blanket over both of us. She tosses her legs to her side, resting her elbow on the armrest.

She doesn't look at me as she extends her arm, wiggling her fingers at me. I can't help the laugh that tumbles past my lips. "Say please, Lea," I chide jokingly.

Her emerald eyes snap to mine as she says, "*Please* give me *my* popcorn that I made."

My lips twitch, but I hand it over. "See? Now, was that so hard?" My voice drops an octave. "All you had to do was ask."

I love how she squirms beside me but refuses to look my way, snatching the remote from between us and starting the movie.

It doesn't take long before her eyes are fluttering shut. Her body starts to slump further into the couch cushions until her feet are completely pressed against my hip.

A faint whistling sound comes out of her before she turns over, stretching herself out in a position that looks less than comfortable. Her head is smooshed into the corner of the couch; she has one leg over my lap, the other bent and digging into my leg.

At nearly six feet tall, she certainly isn't fitting into small spaces like this.

I run my finger up the length of her silky smooth leg. "Lea," I whisper. When she stirs, I speak a bit louder. "Lea, wake up. You're gonna get a kink in your neck."

She sits up, staring at me groggily, but instead of staying upright, she shifts around the couch until her legs are on the opposite side of the couch. She drops her head into my lap and tugs the blanket over her head. A deep sigh puffs past her lips.

This is fine, I tell myself. She'd do this with anyone. You're just a warm body in close proximity and a good pillow. Nothing more. *Stop worrying.*

Despite my thoughts, I can feel my blood pressure start to spike. A twinge of dull pain thrums behind my eye, and acid bubbles in my gut.

Her light strands have fallen over her face, and I resist the urge to brush them away, instead focusing on the way they flutter with each breath she takes.

Loud music drags my attention away, my heart hammering against my chest as Lea burrows further into me. Her arm falls limply in my lap, her fingertips less than an inch from my dick.

I groan, trying to pay attention to the surprisingly well-built Santa on screen who's singing *Jail House Rock* from inside his own jail cell. *How the fuck did he get there?*

My phone buzzes against the wooden end table beside me. I pick it up, hoping it's not my mom or Liam, but I can't be that lucky.

"Hey, Mom," I say, keeping my voice as quiet as possible.

Sobs from her end of the phone have the hair on my neck standing up straight, and my throat feels tight.

"What's wrong?" I ask, my eyes flicking to Lea, hoping like hell she doesn't wake up to hear any of this.

Chapter Thirteen

Lea

Kai's gentle voice starts to trickle into my foggy mind, but when I feel his hand land on my hip, squeezing tightly, his voice grows more strained, and his words come out more quickly.

"Mom, you're okay. I promise," he tells her.

I should sit up so he knows I'm awake. This is none of my business.

I can't make out what his mom is saying, but his body tenses beneath my head with every passing word.

"I know," he says, lowering his voice. "I believe you, Mom. I *really* do. No, no, you are not crazy," he tells her. "Of course, yes. You've been saying he is for a while now, Mom, but you can't let anyone else know that, okay? Promise me you won't tell anyone else."

He releases a long sigh. "I'm going to come see you soon, alright? We'll get it all sorted out. For now, lay low and don't try to contact him again."

Kai's grip on my thigh doesn't relent as the conversation continues, his voice ranging from shrill and panicked to quiet, firm, reassuring. I can't even begin to imagine what they're talking about that has his emotions so all over the place.

"I love you, too, Mom," he tells her, hanging up the phone and dropping it in his lap.

I hear the moment his head hits the back of the worn-out sofa and feel his abs graze my cheek with the long breath he releases.

My eyes flutter open, and I take in his tight lips and clenched-shut eyes. The moment they open and land on me, his nostrils flare.

"How much of that did you hear?" he asks.

"Enough to know you're upset, but not enough to know about what," I admit, my voice small.

He closes his eyes again, sucking in a deep breath, but instead of getting upset with me, his eyes soften when they open. He traces circles along my hip with his fingertip, and the way his cheeks deflate has my heart cramping.

"Do you wanna talk about it?" I ask, not hopeful that he will.

Silence drags between us for several long minutes. Kai closes his eyes, and I can feel some of the anxiety leaching from his body as he draws in a breath through his nose and sighs it out through his mouth.

"My mom has schizophrenia, and she's really bad about staying on her medication. She was calling to tell me that she got into a spat with her neighbors, and they told her she was crazy because she thinks Mel Gibson is speaking to her through the TV."

I sit up, adjusting myself so my legs are in his lap and I'm curled into his side. "I'm sorry, Kai. I had no idea," I tell him. I knew she struggled with her mental health, but my parents never told me more than that, and it didn't feel right to pry it out of Kai growing up. "Why didn't you tell her he's not trying to talk to her?"

He shakes his head, dragging a hand over his face. "I can't, Lea. When people make jokes about being 'delusional', I don't find it funny, and this is exactly why." My neck flushes, and nausea starts to settle into my gut. I have been one of those people, but I won't be going forward, that's for sure. "My mom is actually experiencing delusions and psychosis, and people are out here thinking it's some cute personality trait, but to my mom, she has no fucking clue these things aren't really happening, and telling her differently isn't going to change *her* version of reality."

Kai chews on his lower lip, taking a moment before continuing. "Because for her, these things are very real, and simply telling her it isn't will just agitate her further. It makes her feel like I've turned against her or that someone's pretending to be me."

"I'm sorry, Kai. I can't imagine how stressful that is for you. I admittedly don't know a lot about schizophrenia, but I appreciate you explaining that, and I apologize for ever using the term 'delusional' in the incorrect context."

He stops worrying his lip long enough to face me. Kai presses his forehead against mine, closing his eyes. I wrap my arms around his neck from where I am at his side and apply pressure to one of his earlobes, rolling it between my thumb and forefinger. He groans quietly; some of his stress unfurls from his body.

"Thank you, angel." He breathes quietly, his forehead still pressed to mine. "I'm sorry too," he whispers after another moment.

I pull back from him, my brows drawn together in confusion. "What for?"

His handsome face bears a look of regret, and his tired eyes tug at my heartstrings.

"When you were moving in and you heard me telling Liam I didn't want you here, it isn't what you think," he says. "I was trying to protect you, and honestly, I was—" He scrapes a hand down his face before meeting my eyes again. "I was embarrassed, Lea."

"I'm confused. Embarrassed about what?" *What the hell is he talking about?*

"It's not just my mom. I was diagnosed with schizophrenia during my first year in the AHL after a particularly stressful first season. Stress can be the thing that triggers psychosis, and thanks to Liam, it didn't ruin my future. He knows about my mom, so he got me the help I needed the moment he realized what was happening." My heart swells in appreciation for my brother and his overwhelmingly kind soul. "I'd always worried I'd end up like her, so I didn't handle the diagnosis well at first. Hell, I still don't handle it great, and every goddamn day I worry I've forgotten to take my meds. I recount the pills over and over throughout the day just to be sure I really did. I tried a pill dispenser, but then I just got worried I'd be busy and accidentally take the wrong day's meds and mess it all up."

His admission settles in my gut, and my abdomen clenches around it.

I run my hand down his chest, wrapping it around him to squeeze him tightly to me. I don't think there's much I can say that'll make him feel better, so I opt for comforting him the only way I know how.

We sit in silence, his arms wrapping around me, clutching me tightly to him.

It's surprisingly *nice*.

Until the shrill of my ringer cuts through the silence as the movie credits roll by on the screen.

"It's Liam," I tell Kai, swiping the lock screen and answering the call as I disentangle myself from him.

"Hey, Liam, how's Philly?" I ask, trying to keep my voice even.

"It's good! The team is great. Everyone's been really nice so far too. But I wanted to talk to you about our plans for Christmas..." He trails off, and I already know I'm not going to like what he has to say.

"Go on, hit me with it," I say.

He releases a loud sigh. "We're playing in Vancouver on the twenty-third, and since most of the guys on the team are married, they've decided to bring their wives and kids to spend the holidays there. They asked if I'd wanna tag along, and usually, I wouldn't, but it sounds like fun, and you know I've always wanted to visit Vancouver for more than a game night," he says, practically whining as he does.

"What about Mom and Dad?"

I feel Kai's calloused hand rub along my inner thigh, distracting me for a split second. I smack his hand away, suddenly afraid things between us have become a little too friendly.

"They're both working, Lea. Between finding a new apartment and the move, I haven't been able to send them any money yet, so they need the holiday pay."

My heart sinks to my toes. "Yeah, okay. You should have fun then."

"You sure?"

"Definitely," I say, mustering as much confidence into the word as I can. "Send me tons of pictures."

He chuckles. "I'll try to find a 'Lea' keychain that spells it correctly for you."

"Deal."

"Alright, sis. I've gotta go. We've got a game tonight, but I just wanted to run this by you. Love you."

"I love you too. Have a good game. I'll be watching."

"Thanks, Lea," he says before hanging up.

Kai grabs the remote, swapping back to cable and cueing up the TV for the Philly Scarlets game. Warm-ups should be starting soon.

"Sorry to hear he won't be here for Christmas. I know it's your favorite holiday," Kai says, drawing my attention to him.

Butterflies swarm my stomach at the gravity of his words. *He knows it's my favorite?*

I push the thought away. I've known him my whole life. *Of course* he knows it's my favorite holiday.

"It's fine. I'll just read and watch movies."

He nods, looking unconvinced, and turns his attention back to the TV.

We sit beside each other the rest of the night, not touching again as we watch the game.

The Scarlets win, and when it's over, we head to bed.

Chapter Fourteen

Kai

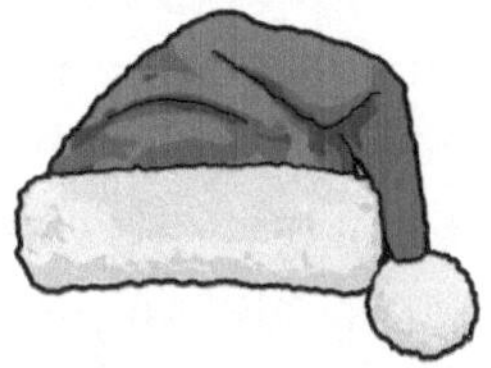

Friday, December 13, 2024

My blades cut through the ice, the last of practice drills running me ragged as I pump my muscles, determined to leave every ounce of frustration I feel toward my situation with Lea on the ice today.

I track the puck as it slides between my teammates, keeping my head on a swivel as I do. I see an opening and signal to Flores so he knows I'm coming for it.

I whip past my teammates, plucking the puck from between them and spraying them with ice as I do, keeping my eyes trained on the net ahead of me. Graham side-checks me, but I don't let it deter me as I send the puck sailing into the net, just an inch from Flores's glove.

Pumping my fist in the air, I let the familiar feeling of adrenaline wash through me, clearing away my earlier anxiety about tonight.

I get a round of high-fives before Coach hollers at us to meet him at center ice.

As a goalie, I rarely get to participate in drills like this. Usually, I'm on the receiving end of the puck, but Coach periodically has us run drills from different positions. It's unconventional, but he swears it gives us a better perspective of what our teammates are doing so we can all be better in sync.

While I definitely feel most at home in the crease, this was a good way to blow off some extra steam.

Especially today.

"Alright, listen up, everyone. Just like every other year, we need a volunteer to dress as Santa for the children's hospital on Christmas Eve."

We all stand in silence, looking between one another for some silent plea that someone will actually volunteer this year.

"You know the drill. If no one volunteers, you'll be voluntold," he scolds.

"Coach," Flores says, dragging our attention to him, but his low brows and the way he slides a hand up his forearm give me no hope that he's offering. "Jessie's due date is the twenty-sixth..." He trails off with no further explanation needed.

The other guys erupt in a chorus of excuses as to why they aren't available either, and Coach's face starts to turn that familiar pink hue before his blazing blue eyes meet mine. "Davis!" he shouts, everyone's attention snapping to me. "I don't see your lips smacking with excuses. You're on this year," he says, clapping his hands with finality. "Now go wash your asses." He dismisses us.

"Coach," I say, a plea clear in my voice. My teammates don't disperse, clearly eager to hear what kind of mess I'll manage to get myself into today. "I don't think there's a Black Santa."

I know damn well I grew up in a home with Black Santas from the 99 Cent Store around the holidays, just like every other New Yorker doing their damndest to diversify their Christmas decor. Coach doesn't need to know that though.

Coach's ears turn bright red, his cheeks puffing as if smoke is about to start blowing out of his nose. "I don't damn well care, and I sure as shit don't think those children will give a flaming fuck either." That's all he says before releasing a loud huff and storming off the ice.

Well, this'll be fun.

Chapter Fifteen

Lea

"**I** can't believe it," I whine to Mona. "Couldn't they have chosen anyone else?"

My best friend's eyes hold no sympathy as she continues applying the dark-red polish to her toes. She glances up at me. "No offense, babe, but you don't have anything going on that day. You said it yourself before practice; your brother will be out of town and your parents are working." She focuses her attention back on her nails. "Besides, isn't it better than being stuck at your apartment with Kai?"

I groan, tossing myself back into the couch cushions. "I guess," I mumble, and I don't miss how her lip quirks on one side.

"Thought so," she chuckles. "Now, get the hell out of my apartment so you and Kai can continue building your slutty empire."

I wave her off, but my pulse thrums in my neck as my cheeks heat.

"Yeah, yeah. I'll see you tomorrow," I tell her, gathering my stuff and waving over my shoulder.

When I arrive home, I hear the shower water running, but as I approach my room, it's coming from *my* shower and not *his*.

I grip the door handle, and the edges of my vision start to blur before I push the door open, letting it slam against the wall.

"Kai!" I shout for him, and the water stops. I hear rustling from inside the bathroom, and the moment he steps out, my heart falls to the floor and my thighs clench together.

His large body is wrapped in nothing but a small white towel tucked around his waist. His umber skin glistens as he leans against the doorframe, crossing his arms over his chest, his corded muscles rippling under my gaze.

I drag my eyes back up his body, meeting his knowing smirk and raised brow. "Something you wanted to say?" he asks, an arrogant laugh leaving those full, biteable lips.

When I don't answer, he tips his chin, assessing me. My voice is caught in my throat as desire manages to snake its way up my spine.

He finally puts me out of my misery, heading back into the bathroom but leaving the door cracked. "My shower wasn't working so I put in a work order, but they won't be here till Monday. I figured you wouldn't want your porn partner to be without a shower," he calls out to me.

When he returns, he's wearing a pair of black sweats and holding my white towel. His muscular arms are covered in tattoos, and they're on full display right now. My mouth waters at the sight of him.

He opens up my closet door, depositing the towel in the basket before facing me again. "You almost ready?" he asks me, and I nod, still unable to speak.

That quirked brow goads me and finally, I manage to croak, "Yep, just need to get set up."

"I'll help. Just tell me what to do," he says.

I nod my chin to the camera bag on my dresser. "You can set the camera up. I've just got to take my meds and then I'll be ready."

His brows pinch together. "You have a migraine coming on? You sure you want to do this?" he asks.

"Yeah, I'm sure." I bite my lip, willing my traitorous nerves not to cause the dreaded word vomit threatening its way up my throat.

"What is it?" he asks, taking a hesitant step toward me.

"Orgasms help—the endorphins, that is," I admit. "That and my affinity for photography are what sparked this idea in the first place." I know it makes it worse for a lot of people with migraines, but it was a happy accident when I learned I'm someone who benefits from it.

Kai blinks slowly, digesting my words, and a slow grin spreads across his lips. Those damned dimples press firmly into his cheeks. "You've got a real triple threat there, angel."

My mouth opens and closes like a fish. "Triple?"

He nods, his grin still firmly in place as he says, "Migraines, photography, and a tight pussy." And just like that, he turns, grabbing my camera bag and getting to work setting it up, leaving me with my mouth agape and my head spinning.

Once the room is all set and I've taken my meds, I grab a light-pink lingerie set and change in the bathroom.

I consider redressing before heading back out, but that'd be useless since I'd just be taking my clothes off in a minute anyway.

I bounce on my toes, shaking my arms out before letting myself out. Tingles erupt throughout my body, and I can't help the wetness already beginning to flood my core.

"You have anything specific in mind?" Kai asks, his eyes still trained on the camera as he adjusts the angle one last time before looking over at me.

His full lips part, and his hands clench briefly before relaxing. Kai drags his eyes slowly down my body, leaving chills in his wake.

"Fuck," he breathes before clearing his throat, dragging us both back to reality.

I head over to him, climbing on the bed and opening the chat room for tonight's video session. "Not really. Sometimes I plan things out, but usually I just have my viewers tell me what they want in the chats."

He nods slowly, his throat working on a swallow. "Yeah—" he stutters. "Sounds good."

"Ready?" I ask, and when he gives me the go-ahead, I check the camera angle one last time, making sure my face can't be seen.

I give him a thumbs up so he knows we're live before starting my usual spiel. "Hello, my little kittens," I purr. "This is Candy Ass, your resident *very bad girl*," I emphasize seductively. "And back by popular demand, we have our special guest from last week. We don't have anything planned for you, so feel free to leave requests in the comments," I tell them.

I flick my gaze over to Kai, who's still standing at the end of the bed. He's biting his lip, and his eyes are glassy.

My tongue darts out to wet my lips, my mouth suddenly feeling dry as we wait for suggestions to pour in.

My hands tremble as I rest them on my abdomen, toying with the lace of my panties. *What if this wasn't a good color? What if I'm too pale for this shade of pink?*

Kai clears his throat, dragging my attention back to him. "You better start checking those messages, angel. I need to touch you," he says, keeping his voice impossibly low, the words sounding strained.

My thighs part, and a ragged breath leaves my lungs before I manage to flick my attention back on the screen.

"What do our viewers want, angel?" he taunts, and my mouth waters as he strokes his bulge through his sweats.

"They—" I suck in a breath. "They want to see you too," I tell him.

His head rears back, and his brows cinch in confusion.

I quickly mute the mic.

"We can do whatever you're comfortable with. I have masks in my nightstand if you want to show more of yourself, or you could just show your dick or nothing at all. You can even walk away right now. The puck is on your ice," I tell him, ensuring he knows that no matter what, consent remains a priority.

He shakes himself out of it, squeezing his eyes closed for a moment before saying, "Where are the masks?"

My pulse quickens, and I feel breathless. I have no idea how far we're planning to take this tonight, but I can't wait to find out.

"Top drawer," I say, pointing to the wooden nightstand to my right. Kai sifts through the drawer, and I write a comment to my viewers to let them know we'll be right back after we reposition the camera.

He plucks the two lacey masks from the drawer, holding them up high as they dangle from his fingers. "You *cannot* be fucking serious right now," he deadpans.

"It's that or nothing," I say, rolling my eyes and extending my hand for him to pass me one.

Instead of dropping the hot-pink mask in my hand, he keeps that for himself and gives me the black one before securing it to his face.

"Good call." I smirk. "Pink might just be your color."

His brown eyes dance with mischief as he trails a hand down his body. "Are you kidding? *Every* color is *my* color. Have you seen me? I'm a work of art," he says with a cocky smirk.

He's not wrong.

"Alright, angel. Get the hell back on the bed. I wouldn't want to leave our viewers waiting too long," he jokes as he moves the camera further from the bed to allow for a wider frame.

I shake my head, dropping to my knees several feet from the bed. Kai's jaw clenches, and he drags a hand down his face, understanding exactly what I'm asking for.

Once we're live again, Kai takes a seat on the very edge of the mattress, pointing a finger at me and crooking it toward him.

I sit up on my knees, crawling toward him, and have to work to keep the saliva pooling in my mouth from running over.

"Such a good girl," he says, running his fingers through my hair and gripping my roots tightly at the nape of my neck, dragging my head back. He forces me to look up at him, and my eyes zero in on the way he sucks on his lower lip.

Kai glances away for a moment before meeting my eyes again. "Take it out," he instructs, his voice remaining low and raspy.

My hands rest on his hips as I hook my fingers into the waistband of his sweatpants and drag them down his powerful thighs as he lifts his ass to help me. His cock springs free, and a quiet gasp passes my lips.

"Pretty impressive, huh?" he asks, that cocky attitude of his on full display.

I don't even have it in me to deny it or try to take him down a peg or two. No, instead, my body betrays me.

My core coils, my breath leaving me in pants as I carve every detail of this moment into my brain.

This is only the second time I've seen his dick, and somehow, it's even more incredible than the first time.

I glance up at him and ask, "Can I use my mouth?" My words come out as a desperate plea, but I couldn't care less. If I really need to justify this behavior later, I'll just say it was all for show.

Not that Kai, nor his ego, would believe that anyway.

"Well, since you asked so nicely. I think I can allow that," he says, but before I can move my mouth, he's already using the hand in my hair to guide me to him.

I fucking *love* that he's taking control and owning this.

My lips wrap around the head of his engorged length, my tongue swiping the precum beading from the tip. The salty liquid coats my mouth, and a moan fills my throat, *as does Kai.*

My hands remain on his hips, balancing so I don't literally impale myself on him.

He groans loudly, thrusting into my face. "That's it, angel. Fuck, you take me so well," he says, his praise shooting straight to my clit.

His fingers loosen in my hair, slipping down the column of my throat. He presses his thumb firmly on the base of my neck, causing me to gag around him as I take him even more deeply, my eyes burning as I do.

"Fuck, yes," he groans, and I feel his thick length continue to swell on my tongue.

Jesus Christ.

My body aches to be touched, and I feel lightheaded, both from lack of oxygen and the overwhelming feeling of Kai.

He squeezes my neck, grunting as his body stills. I pull back, peering up at him for permission to keep going.

His head is tossed back, eyes clenched shut and nostrils flared as he sucks in a deep, steadying breath.

When his eyes finally find mine, they're blazing, and my legs are trembling with the effort it takes to hold myself up.

"My turn, angel. On your hands and knees," he says, pulling me up by my biceps, not waiting for me to obey.

I turn over on shaking limbs.

The moment I'm positioned how he wants, his warm hands are on my hips, gliding down to my ass cheeks. He takes big handfuls, squeezing firmly.

"Someday, I'm going to take your ass too," he warns. One of his hands leaves me, but only briefly before landing with a loud *thwack*.

A jolt of pleasure and pain rears through me, and I collapse onto my forearms.

His calloused fingers dip into the fabric of my pink thong, dragging it down my ass. "I love this color on you." He hums, and his words are so quiet it feels like they're meant solely for my ears.

I preen under his attention, my abdomen flowing with molten lava as he removes my panties. I feel his hot breath on one globe before his teeth scrape across the skin.

My knees part further, widening my stance on instinct for him.

"Please," I whine.

"So damn greedy." He tsks. His hands slide down the outside of my thighs. I watch on my laptop screen as he lowers himself behind me, and my muscles coil tightly with anticipation.

"Tell me if you need a break," he whispers before his mouth is on me.

"Oh!" I gasp, my eyes widening as he draws my pussy lips into his mouth, sucking me between his teeth, moving the pad of his thumb over my clit and applying a delicious pressure.

"You like that?" he asks, his words muffled with his head still between my legs.

"God, yes!" I cry, my clit pulsating under the delicious pressure he's creating with his thumb and forefinger as he pinches and rubs me.

My hips buck into his face, my thighs shaking. "I'm gonna come," I moan, my eyes rolling to the back of my head.

"That's it, angel. Come on my fucking face," Kai grinds out. He continues sucking and flicking his tongue, hastening his pace as I cry out.

"Fuck! Yes, yes, yes," I whimper, my voice sounding impossibly needy as euphoria surges through me, lighting up each of my nerve endings.

My pulse is bounding, and my chest is heaving with each breath I take as I fall slowly back to earth in Kai's capable hands.

Chapter Sixteen

Kai

I sit up, wiping my hand down my face to collect all of Lea's juices. God, this woman is driving me fucking wild. Her pretty pussy, soft skin, and all that silvery-white hair are a dangerous combination.

I wrap her hair around my palm, pulling her up so her back is against my chest and she's sitting up on her shins. I don't even look at the screen before telling her, "Our viewers want me inside you, angel." *Truth be told, I don't give a single fuck about what they want.*

She nods in agreement, clearly eager for me to fill her under the guise of it being for those watching. Unfortunately for Lea, I'm fully aware that she'd be begging me for my dick with or without the cameras on.

I snake a hand around her waist, cupping her breast and twisting her nipple, rubbing my thumb over it to soothe the sting each time.

She's writhing against me, her body shaking as her needy little pussy practically begs to be filled. "You want that, don't you, angel? You want to feel me buried deep inside you."

"Yes," she moans, the word sounding breathless.

"Today's your lucky day then. I'm feeling charitable, and I happen to be in a unique position to help someone in need right now," I tell her, my lips grazing the shell of her ear.

Her hands claw into my thighs as she grits out, "I swear to god, if you don't fuck me right now, I'll do it myself with a toy that'll be even more satisfying than you could ever be." She lets out a huff before adding, "And I'll make you watch."

My hand wraps around her throat, pressing until I see her breaths come out in smaller, quicker bursts as her lungs beg for oxygen. "First, don't ever threaten me again, and second," I say, tightening my grip one last time, "don't ever fucking lie to me." I release my hold on her throat before pushing her down onto the mattress. When she falls forward, I grip her hips, flipping her over onto her back.

I glare down at her needy body, her lips parted, pupils blown wide, and strands of that platinum hair stuck to her face. She looks like a mess and I fucking *love it*. I lower myself over her, covering her body with my own and allowing the tip of my dick to graze her slickness. My hands bracket her face as I say, "You and I both know I'm about to ruin you for every other man, and before the night is up, you're going to be begging for me to take control and let you lose yourself in me."

"God, I hate you," she groans, but the way she maintains eye contact with me and the needy way her hips grind against me, silently pleading for more of me, gives her away.

I lower my head, breaking eye contact with her for a brief second and releasing a humorless laugh as I do. When my gaze returns to her green glossy eyes, I can't help but smirk. "No, angel. No, you fucking don't."

Her teeth sink into her plump bottom lip, her eyes full of need as she runs her hands up my chest.

"Just shut up and fuck me," she cries.

A loud groan rips through my throat, and my hand slips between us, gripping the base of my dick. "You still okay with no condom?" I ask her, confirming what we'd discussed when Lea and I went over all the rules of our agreement before having started this.

We both get tested regularly thanks to our contracts with the AHL, and she's on the pill.

"Yes," she whimpers, and the sound goes straight to my dick.

I line myself up with her, rubbing the head of my dick through her slick heat before plunging in.

My vision goes blurry, and all the air is stolen from my lungs as I seat myself inside her. My ass cheeks clench, and a tremor wracks through me.

Lea's back arches off the bed, and her head falls back, exposing her neck to me as she moans and mumbles incoherently.

"Good?" I ask, panting as I begin thrusting into her, playing with how much of me I'm willing to remove before I press back into her.

"So good," she cries, digging her fingers into my skin.

I want to watch her take her fill. I want her to come around my dick, using me to get her there.

I move a hand to her hip and use the other to brace myself on the bed, gripping her as I roll over, remaining inside her as I flip her to sit on top of me.

Her hands bolt out, steadying herself on my chest as she stares down at me with wide eyes.

"Go on, angel. Take your fill. Do your job, and make us both come," I tell her, lying back with my head resting on my crossed forearms.

Her bottom lip quivers as she nods, lowering herself onto me and back up. My fingertips tingle with the need to touch her, but I resist, allowing myself the simple pleasure of watching this gorgeous woman fuck herself with my dick.

Her little tits bounce as she lifts herself before sinking back down on me. My dick is screaming for me to just fill her with my load, but I'm holding back. My jaw is clenched so tight as I focus on the task at hand that I'm worried I might crack a fucking tooth.

"Just a little more, angel. Don't you want me to fill you up?"

She nods weakly, her chin wobbling as she works herself onto me. I Kegel inside her, and her eyes shoot open with a loud gasp.

"Answer the question, angel. Do you want me to fill your tight pussy with my cum? I'm more than happy to since you've been such a good girl this year. You can consider it your Christmas present," I taunt.

Her legs shake as she cries out, a flood of her sticky heat coating my dick as she continues pretending not to love this as much as she does.

"You need some help?" I offer, my tone teasing.

She shakes her head adamantly. "No," she gasps out. "I'm fine," she adds, whimpering.

This unspoken game is seconds from having me on my knees, begging for her mercy, but judging by the sheen of sweat coating her brow, I know I'm about to win.

Any second now.

Lea falls forward onto my chest as she rocks her body back and forth against my hips with me still fully lodged inside her. "It's so fucking good," she grinds out. "The best I've ever had," she whines. "Please fuck me; I need it," she breathes, then corrects herself. "I need *you*."

Pride fills my chest. "Now, was that so hard?" I ask, rolling us over one more time before I bury my face in her neck, my senses overflowing with her sweet vanilla scent. *Just like a damn sugar cookie.*

I drive my hips into her; the sound of her cries and our hips slapping together fills the room, and as she writhes against me, I lose it.

All sense of control is thrown out the window.

My movements become more erratic, all rhythm lost as Lea's pussy tightens around me.

Her pulse pounds in her neck, and I watch as she comes undone around me, screaming and panting. The moment my brain registers that she's coming, I'm busting my nut inside her, filling her up with my cum as heat blazes through me and tendrils of electricity zip up my spine.

I settle onto her, careful not to totally crush her under my bulk.

Lea blinks rapidly, clearing the lusty haze from her eyes before leaning over to the laptop. "Thanks," she says, exhaustion evident in her tone. "Thanks for watching, my little kittens. We'll see you back next week," she says before slamming her laptop shut and collapsing back against the mattress.

She drapes an arm over her face, her breath coming out ragged as we both work to calm our breathing.

I grip her cheeks in my hand, squishing her lips together as I direct her face to mine. "You're mine now, Lea."

I drop my hand, sliding out of her. Her lips part, and suddenly, I have another idea.

I gather her limp body in my arms, rolling over onto my side and positioning my now semi-erect dick at her entrance. She grips my forearm. "I don't think I can handle anymore," she whines.

My hand slips between her legs resting over her clit. I swirl my fingertips lazily, and her thighs part again. She sucks in another breath and lets her head roll back against my shoulder. "Are you sure, angel?" I whisper.

"Maybe just one m–" she groans loudly when I slip myself inside her, and my dick rapidly hardens as she clenches around me again. "You know what? Do whatever you want. Clearly, you know best," she says, her voice snarky, and it makes me laugh.

We lay like this for a while. Neither of us particularly chasing the orgasm, just enjoying the ride to get there. When we come this time, my hand is wrapped around her thigh, pulling her knee toward my chest. Her moans are softer, and it doesn't hit us all at once this time, but small ripples of electricity tunnel through me, and when we're done, we just lie here for a while longer.

When I finally extract myself from her body, she flops back on the mattress, groaning as she does.

I get up and head to her shower to get washed off, hoping like hell she follows me in there. It only takes a few minutes to wash and dry myself, slipping back into my gray sweats as I traipse back into her room. Lea is spread out like a starfish on her bed, unmoving.

"You okay there, Leonora?" I ask, chuckling as I pass by her.

She sticks up the arm that's not covering her face and shoots me a thumbs up.

"I'm gonna order pizza. Get your ass up and shower if you want to eat because I'm not saving you any," I say, leaving the room for her to gather herself.

That's another lie though. *I'd save her the whole damn pizza and beg for her crumbs if I thought it'd make her happy.*

Chapter Seventeen
Kai

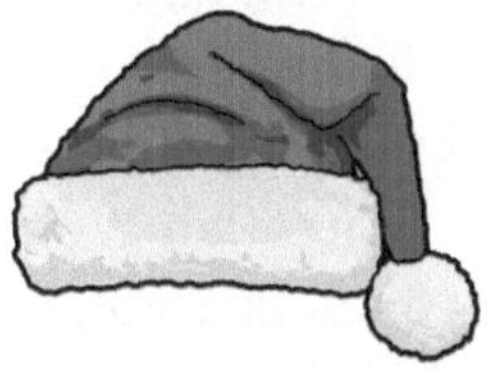

Wednesday, December 18, 2024

I sit on the edge of the couch, ready to tackle her if she reaches a point where she might hurt herself or someone else.

My mom paces her small trailer, the floor covered in trash, and her hands tremble as she speaks aimlessly.

"Mom," I say, keeping my voice steady as I try to propel all the confidence that I'm definitely *not* feeling into the word.

She spins to face me, her wide eyes locking on mine for a split second before she shakes her head, her eyes darting around the room, and the rambling continues.

"Mom, you've got to take your pill. I promise it's *okay*. I'll take one too," I tell her, hoping I can at least get a single dose in her.

Her long, matted ash brown hair hangs down her back, bouncing with each step she takes. "Pill? I will take a pill," she says, not looking at me.

Unlike when I was a kid, there's no hope that gets lodged in my throat, just waiting for her to crush me again when she doesn't follow through. No, *now I know better.*

She starts rambling, the clang associations starting from the top. "Pill, I will take a pill, but I can't sit still because if I sit still, my name might be Jill, and if *I'm Jill,* then who would kill Will?"

She's not going to kill anyone, but unfortunately, for whoever this "Will" fucker is, both his name and kill rhyme with pill.

Christ. I blow out a defeated lungful of air through my nose before plucking my phone from my back pocket.

I check my bank account, happy to see that things are going well with our "viewers." After last Friday's show, Lea and I made *three times* what we had the first time I joined her.

I was hoping to use the money to give myself a little financial cushion and repay some of that loan, but I think this is the last straw for me. She needs to be somewhere with trained professionals who can keep her safe, make sure she's taking her medication, and provide the mental health services she desperately needs.

Watching my mother pace this disgusting home, unconsolable and unaware of who I am or where she's at, has acid settling in the pit of my stomach.

My muscles cramp, and I'm having difficulty swallowing my saliva as the smell of rotten food wafts up my nose. *Or maybe that's just her.*

Bile rises up my throat, but I push it down, focusing on the task ahead of me.

My thumbs work quickly on my phone screen, searching for the best way to get her help.

It looks like I have two options: I could call the police and have them admit her against her will. Calling the police doesn't feel like a real option, though, not for me.

Or I can bring her to the emergency room and have them admit her.

My hand cups the back of my neck, squeezing as I focus on taking regular breaths.

I look up at my mom, her pale, wrinkled face pinched in distress, and dread fills my chest.

No matter how we do this, it has to happen.

I barely register the sound of the front door opening as I sit here, unmoving, and staring slack-jawed at the wall.

I don't know when I finally made it home after seeing my mom, but I haven't been able to form a coherent thought since.

Nausea roils through me, unrelenting.

"Kai?" A voice wiggles its way through the periphery of my walls, drawn up tightly around me.

"Kai, are you okay?"

There's shuffling around me, the couch dips beside me, and when something warm and tight wraps around my upper body, I flinch, everything falling back into place suddenly.

My wide eyes meet Lea's as she looks up at me with a startled expression.

"Kai, is everything alright?" she asks, keeping her voice quiet as if she doesn't want to spook me further.

I shake my head slowly. "I don't think so," I say, blowing a breath slowly past my lips.

She runs a soothing palm up and down my spine, stopping at the base to rub circles there. "Do you want to talk about it?" she asks, her voice gentle, quiet.

I'm not sure anyone besides Liam has ever asked me that.

My words get lodged in my throat as I fight to hold back the tears welling in my eyes. *Do I want to talk about it?*

"It's okay if you don't. I just want you to know I'm here..." she says, her voice trailing off.

We sit in silence for a few long moments as my raging pulse finally begins to slow in her presence.

My mouth feels dry when I finally open it to speak. "It's my mom." That's all I manage at first, dipping my toes in and testing the water to see how it feels to open up to someone besides her brother. A pang of guilt hits me when I think of Liam. God, he'd be pissed about what we've been doing together.

"Is she okay?"

I shake my head. "Not really," I croak out and feel like an asshole for not giving her more details yet. I don't *want* her to worry. It's just so hard to talk about this.

"It's okay," she says, resting her head on my shoulder. "Take your time, Kai."

I nod slowly, dragging in a few deep breaths and willing the ache in my chest to relent. "Things have gotten worse since I'd last seen her—" I gulp more air. "Since I picked her up from jail."

She sucks in an audible breath. "Jail?"

I clench my eyes shut and feel the moisture coat my lashes, making it difficult to see when I open my eyes again.

"She had done something that got her arrested, and I had to bail her out. That's why I agreed to join you. I needed to take out a loan to pay it because my savings from the league have all been spent on rent, copays for my medication so I don't wind up like her, and bailing her out of jail and keeping a roof over her head." The admission feels sour on my tongue, but I'm glad it's out there. It sucks having to keep this heavy shit bottled up.

Lea places a hand on my cheek, drawing my eyes to hers. They're filled with sympathy. "I'm sorry you've had to deal with all of this alone," she says, her voice impossibly small.

"Liam used to help, but he's not here anymore, and I know he'd want me to tell him, but I don't want anything distracting him. He's finally living out our dream, and one day, I'll be there to join him." I huff out another breath that had been caught in my lungs. "I've just got to make it through this shit first."

Lea's thumb strokes my cheekbone softly, and she gives me a small, reassuring smile.

"If that was a few weeks ago, what happened to-day?" she asks.

My hand lands on her wrist, squeezing it gently as she cradles my cheek in her palm. I rub small circles along her pulse, allowing the strong, steady beat to soothe me.

A tight band of pain feels like it's wrapped around my forehead, and there's a pounding in my temples.

"I hadn't heard from her in a couple of days, so I went to check in on her and found her in her trailer. It was filled with trash and rotting food. She looked and smelled like she hadn't showered in weeks and couldn't form coherent sentences."

Lea nods, not saying anything as she allows me time to find my words.

"She was past the point of my help, so I had to have her admitted to an inpatient psychiatric hospital. She didn't go willingly, so the doctor who saw her in the ER had to petition for a fifty-one fifty, which is an involuntary psychiatric hold for up to one hundred and twenty hours. It means that she can't just check herself out of the hospital because she's considered a danger to herself or others right now."

Lea trails her hand down the side of my neck, resting it in my lap and giving my thigh a squeeze.

"I'm so sorry, Kai," she says, her voice cracking on a watery sound. "I can't possibly imagine how difficult that must've been for you to see her like that. You did the right thing for her, but sometimes that's so hard," she says, grasping my hand and bringing it to her mouth to press a gentle kiss to my palm.

My heart cracks wide open.

"It's really fucking hard," I say, and the admission has tears freely flowing.

As a Black man in America, especially playing a predominantly white sport, I usually feel like I have to bottle things up. I don't feel safe expressing a full range of emotions for fear of judgment or worse, so sitting here with Lea, feeling completely safe to do so—it has a lot of things stirring in my chest. Many of which I'm unfamiliar with.

Chapter Eighteen

Lea

Sitting with Kai as he admits things I'd have never guessed about him has a strange sensation of gratitude settling in my gut.

The fact that he feels comfortable enough with me to allow me to see this side of him is something I won't take for granted.

My eyes feel misty, and my lip wobbles as I try to hold myself together.

This isn't about me.

I wouldn't dare do anything to make this moment about *me*.

"Do you have any idea how long it'll be before she's out? Maybe I can help you get things at her trailer settled so she's ready to come home when she's better?"

He gives me a tight smile that doesn't reach his eyes. "I don't know how long it'll be, but I'd appreciate that," he says, his voice impossibly small when he speaks those last words.

"Whatever you need, just tell me, okay?"

He nods, wrapping his arms around my waist and hoisting me into his lap. I melt into him, trailing my hands up his chest and around his neck.

"I'm scared," he whispers. His chin is trembling, and I feel his body shaking around me.

I tuck myself firmly against him, trying to ground his body with my own.

"She's getting the help she needs, and that's because of *you*, Kai."

"I just"— he shakes his head—"I don't want to end up like her, Lea," he says, his voice breaking on a near-sob as he tucks his face into the side of my neck. The wetness from his tears is slick on my throat, and it's like a punch to the gut to see this strong, capable, confident man so upset.

"You won't, Kai," I tell him, projecting as much confidence as I can muster into my voice as I stroke his short, coarse hair.

"You can't know that, Lea," he breathes. "I worry every damn day that I'll forget a dose of my meds or that I won't be able to afford them and I'll slowly start to lose my mind."

"I hear you," I whisper. "I do, but let's just take it one day at a time, okay?"

He nods, unspeaking, as we sit here in silence until the sun has set and the living room of our tiny apartment is cloaked in darkness.

Chapter Nineteen

Lea

Thursday, December 19, 2024

"Kai," I whisper, shaking his shoulder to wake him.

His blinks are slow as he starts to shift under me, stretching out his long limbs after a night spent on this tiny loveseat.

Once his eyes focus on me, he gives me a small, embarrassed smile. One I'm certain I've never seen on his face before.

This is a man who exudes smug confidence, but I'm beginning to think a lot of that is a cover for how he's really feeling.

"Good morning, angel," he says, shifting beneath me.

This hard bulge he's sporting glides between my thighs as I continue to straddle him, my eyes widening as a jolt of pleasure strikes me.

No, Lea. Bad, Lea! No sexy time.

I shift off of him so he can sit up. "I've gotta shower and get dressed. I was voluntold I'd be dressing as Mrs. Claus this year for the children's hospital." I roll my eyes. "Who was chosen from your team?"

Each year, there's a Mrs. Claus chosen from the female AHL team and Santa from the men's.

When Kai doesn't answer, I turn to face him. His coffee-brown eyes are dancing with mischief, and a wide grin splits his face. "You're lookin' at him, angel."

My mouth falls open, and I smack my palm to my forehead, groaning.

Looks like we'll be spending the holidays together after all.

Not that that would be such a terrible thing. Though I'm already feeling myself becoming more attached to him by the day, and the idea of seeing him interact with children, even if he *was* voluntold, makes my stomach flutter with butterflies.

Kai stands from the couch, prowling toward me. He bends forward, wrapping his strong arms around my waist, and hauls me over his shoulder.

I release a yelp, smacking at his back. "Kai! Put me down!"

His warm palm squeezes my ass, and heat threads through me. "No can do, *Leonora.* We've got an appointment to make, and I don't want us wasting any water. It would be bad for the planet," he says, carrying me into my bathroom and setting me down on the cool countertop.

I watch with anticipation as he tugs his shirt off, dropping it to the floor. He leans into the shower, turning the faucet on before facing me.

"Start undressing, angel. If I have to do it for you, there'll be a price to pay." His eyes hold a wicked glint in them, and my core clenches, my knees parting slightly of their own accord.

Part of me wants to defy him and find out what my punishment would be, but the needier part of me wins out, wanting him inside me as quickly as possible.

I hop off the counter, wrenching my shirt over my head and unclasping my bra, letting it slide down my arms and to the floor. My fingers hook in the waistband of my shorts and panties, dragging them down my legs.

I step out of them, and Kai grips my hips, hoisting me up his body. I wrap my legs firmly around his hips, his cock nudging my entrance as he carries me into the shower with him.

Warm water flows over us, and my pulse quickens, my thighs clenching around him.

He presses my back against the cold shower tile and aligns the head of his dick with me. "No fore-play?" I ask jokingly.

He quirks a dark brow, the corner of his lip turning up in a lopsided smirk. "Angel, you're so goddamn wet for me right now. I can feel it dripping down your thighs. Besides, we don't have time," he says, chuckling as he slides into me. His laughter stops abruptly, replaced by a low groan.

"God, you're so fucking warm," he moans.

My arms tighten around his neck, my muscles burning as I try to hold myself up, but his thick length pushing slowly into me leaves my muscles quivering and my mouth watering.

"It feels too good." I moan, letting my head fall back against the tile.

His hips jerk once his cock is fully seated in me. Kai buries his face in my neck, sucking on the sensitive skin at the base of my throat.

Tingles erupt throughout my body, my pussy walls clenching around him.

He grips my wrists, holding them against the wall on either side of my head. My legs wobble around him, my ankles crossing in an effort to remain around him. "I can't, Kai. It's too much. I can't hold on," I cry out.

His thrusts become unrelenting. "You can and you will, angel. I'll have you there any second, baby. Just hold on," he grunts.

I drop one of my legs, balancing on my toes, and he allows me to rest for just a moment before yanking my leg back up and around his waist.

My vision blurs and my nipples tighten against the feel of his sparse chest hair rubbing against me.

This is the first time we've ever been fully naked together, and instead of feeling exposed, I feel *worshiped*.

"Yes," I moan. "God, yes! Just like that," I whine.

"Wrong three-letter name, angel. *Try again*," he says, his tone warning as he nips my earlobe.

Warmth floods my core, the muscles in my abdomen coiling, and when Kai leaves me completely, my breath gets caught in my throat, only for him to thrust all the way in.

"Kai!" I scream.

"Yes, angel. Just like that. *Say my name.*"

Euphoria wracks through my body, and I spasm around him, tumbling back to earth.

"Kai," I continue to moan.

"Such a good fucking girl," he groans. "Your tight pussy takes me so well."

I feel him stiffen inside me, my pussy still spasming around him in waves. He releases a low groan, his forehead falling to mine as his movements become unrestrained, and his own orgasm shatters through his body.

His hot cum fills me, and when he slides out of me, I feel it running down my thighs with my own arousal.

I suck a deep breath in and teeter forward when he helps me unfold myself from his body, blood rushing back to my limbs. The feeling of pins and needles leaves me unsteady on my feet, but Kai holds me firmly in his arms.

Several minutes pass as we regain control of our breathing, and Kai removes the shower head, spinning me around so he can stand at my back. He runs the hot water over my body, rinsing away the stickiness gathered between my legs before he pumps my body wash into his hands, working it into a lather.

He cleans my body, moving on to wash and condition my hair, even combing my knotted waves out before I move on to him.

The water runs down his chiseled chest, the coarse, dark curls of his chest hair tickling my fingertips as I lather his body.

When we're both rinsed off, we towel dry and get changed before heading to our costume fitting.

Chapter Twenty

Kai

Friday, December 20, 2024

The last game before we're off for the holidays leaves my body run ragged. I put everything I had into it, and it paid off.

We won, and now I'm looking forward to doing the same with Lea.

I make my way into our apartment, stopping to pick up a package left by the door. Confusion draws my brows together as I read the name on the package. It's addressed to me.

"I haven't ordered anything," I mutter to myself as I make my way inside.

Lea's door is open, and I see her lying in bed with her lamp on, probably reading something smutty like she usually is.

"Leonora, I'm home," I call out to her, and she drops her book in her lap, a wide smile beaming at me.

"Hey! Good game tonight," she says, and my heart soars in my chest.

"Thanks. I'll be back out in a second. I'm just gonna get changed and we can get started."

She nods, picking up her book and placing a bookmark inside before closing it and setting it on her nightstand.

"Sounds good. I'll start getting everything set up how we spoke about," she says, standing from her bed.

I dump my gear in the hall closet and head to my room, stripping out of my shirt and changing into a long sleeve.

I'm just about ready to meet Lea in her room, but the package I brought in sits on my dresser, staring at me.

I tear into it, curious as to what I ordered that I might've forgotten, and when I see what's in the clear bag inside the package, my heart stops.

A dizzy feeling knocks into me, forcing me to take a seat on the edge of the bed as I unwrap the pill bottles.

There's a light knock on my door, and Lea pokes her head inside, giving me a small smile. "Hey, I'm ready when you are," she says, her voice quietly floating around me. Her eyes land on the bottles in my hands, and her smile widens a fraction before she takes a seat beside me, pressing a chaste kiss on my cheek.

I don't know when or how we got to this point, but her casual touches leave my throat thick with unspoken words.

"They're cool, right? A pretty simple solution to a common problem," she tells me. "You just transfer your pills to these bottles, or if the caps fit, you can just swap those out. The timer on the top counts the amount of time it's been since you last opened it, and resets when you close it again. This way, you won't have to recount your pills ten times a day or worry that you missed a dose."

The bottles fall out of my grasp, rolling onto the floor. I wrap my arms around Lea, clutching her body to mine.

She releases a little rasp, tapping my back. "Can't breathe," she manages, and I loosen my hold on her.

My eyes meet her mossy-green ones, holding her attention as I whisper, "Thank you." My throat is hoarse, and the words sound strained and unfamiliar.

"Don't mention it, big guy," she says, clearing her throat as she stands from my lap.

"Come on, you've gotta shake that money maker," she jokes, a giggle slipping past her lips.

The sound lights me up inside and I obey, my legs carrying me after her and into her room.

"So, you've sort of broken me," she says, her cheeks turning a pretty pink hue as she looks sheepishly away, suddenly unable to make eye contact with me. "And you just played a long game, plus it's super late anyway, so I figured we could just do some mutual masturbation and make this a fast one. I'm exhausted after practice this morning, and I think I pulled something at my game last night."

"Whatever you want," I tell her, my mind already plotting out all the ways I can take care of her tired muscles when we're done. She deserves a bath, a massage, and some hot and cold cream.

Her eyes flash back to mine, heat simmering behind them as she strips out of her blue cotton shorts and matching t-shirt.

My mouth starts to water, and my dick swells in my shorts, and just as quickly, they're on the ground.

"On the bed, big guy." She smirks.

"Yes, ma'am," I say, climbing onto one side.

She does the same, draping a leg over mine and spreading her muscular thighs wide for the camera. I can't help but lean over her to get a good look, and sure enough, her arousal is already dripping from her pussy, soaking the red lace, held up by a matching garter.

I suck my bottom lip between my teeth, holding in a groan as I lean back onto her fluffy white pillows. My rough hand wraps around the base of my dick, tugging as she gets the chat cued up.

"We're on in three seconds," she whispers to me, and all I can do is nod.

"Hello, my little kittens, and a very slutty little holiday season to everyone who celebrates," she says cheerfully. Her eyes land on my dick, watching as I stroke myself. She clears her throat, covering her mouth with her fist to muffle the sound. "Clearly, *someone* couldn't wait any longer," she finally jokes.

"We apologize for the late hour, but our guest here had some things to attend to. I assure you, we'll make it worth the wait though."

Her eyes scan the chat room, and she picks a few comments to read, ending on one that has me gripping my dick too tight and my nostrils flaring as she reads, "Fred wants to know if we'll be allowing high tippers to speak tonight," she announces, looking over at me.

My lips are pinched tight at the thought of her coming to the sound of another man's voice.

"How about we allow it, but—" She watches my face intently as she hesitates. I give her a curt nod, trying to remind myself what it is we're *really* doing here. "All tips have to be five hundred dollars or higher if you want to speak."

My jaw nearly drops. *Who the fuck is going to tip that much just to speak to us?*

I guess we're about to find out.

Lea leans back, threading her fingers into mine. A hand slips between her legs, and she toys with her clit first, rubbing small, firm circles on the swollen pink bud.

Her middle finger dips inside, drawing out her wetness. The slick sound of her finger sliding inside her, *where I should be right now*, has my throat closing and my muscles feeling loose.

A loud ding sounds from her laptop, and a muffled voice comes through the speakers, sounding crackly. "Candy Ass, this is Larry," the voice says, and my legs begin to shake with annoyance.

"Hi, Larry," Lea purrs. "Thank you *so much* for the tip."

"You're welcome," he says, and a long, deep cough leaves him before he recovers. "Can we see you stroke your guest's cock? I wanna see you squeeze the tip until there's precum," he tells her.

My eyes widen in shock at his request.

Is he fucking kidding?

Lea giggles beside me. "Of course, Larry," she tells him, untangling her fingers from mine as one hand remains on her pussy and the other wraps around my shaft.

She gives it a long, slow pump from tip to base and back up that has all the air leaving my lungs in a huff and my eyes rolling back. When she gets to my tip, she rolls her thumb over the head, then chokes up on it until two small beads of precum spill out the tip.

I groan loudly, and Lea swipes her thumb through the moisture, bringing it to her mouth and sucking it off. She moans, and her eyes roll back. I know it isn't just for show because these people can't see anything besides her pussy. Her thumb leaves her mouth with a loud "pop," and my dick twitches in my palm.

Money floods in, and more men and one woman take their turns giving us instructions, speaking to Lea like she's theirs.

I can feel the vein in my temple pulsing with anger, and when Lea finally comes, the sound is like a beacon to my dick. My orgasm hits me hard and fast through the rage surging through my blood, and the moment it's over and she's thanked every-one, I'm out of this room and in my shower. *Alone.*

An hour or more passes before I hear Lea knock lightly on my door, but I don't answer.

And just like usual, she doesn't fucking listen, barging into my room and flopping down beside me in bed.

"I'm not sure what's going on, but clearly, you're upset about something. If you're not careful, those veins in your neck might pop," she says, chuckling as she pulls my blanket over herself.

I let out a long huff. "I don't wanna have to hear other people speaking to you like you're theirs," I admit.

She runs a hand up and down my forearm. "But I'm not theirs, Kai. *I'm all yours.*"

It isn't enough, but *for now*, it'll have to be.

We lie in silence, nothing but our breaths filling the room around us as we wait for the other to speak.

Lea gives in first, her voice impossibly small as she says, "Hey, Kai."

"Yes, Leonora?" I ask, working to sound annoyed, but there's no bite behind my words.

"I was thinking that maybe tomorrow we could go work on cleaning out your mom's trailer so it's ready for her."

My heart clenches in my chest, my ribs contract-ing painfully with each breath I take.

I clear the lump from my throat before answering, "Sure, angel. That'd be good."

Chapter Twenty-One

Lea

Saturday, December 21, 2024

We should've brought hazmat suits.

When Kai told me it was bad the other day, I hadn't been prepared for just *how* bad. We've been working in here for hours with the doors and windows open, trying to air the place out and hoping the flies would leave too as we fill trash bag after trash bag with garbage.

"I spoke with the doctor overseeing her inpatient management yesterday morning," Kai says, looking over his shoulder at me as he bends to stuff empty soda cans in a bag.

"Yeah? How's she doing?"

"Good, actually. He says she has a long way to go and can't give me a timeline just yet, but he says after the holidays, so long as things continue the way they have been, she'll be allowed visitors."

My heart swells, and my hand absentmindedly slips over my chest, clutching the small silver pendant that's hanging around my neck.

"That's incredible, Kai," I tell him, turning my attention back to the massive stack of boxes he has me clearing out.

"Thanks, Lea," he says, his voice barely above a whisper.

Another hour passes by the time I make it to the bottom of the pile. I take a seat on the couch, dragging it into my lap and slipping my fingers under the lip.

Please don't be a dead mouse, please don't be a dead mouse, I chant in my head.

It wouldn't be the first time today.

A thin layer of dust covers the folded letters inside.

My brows furrow in confusion, but I decide to close the box since there's nothing to clean up. A name on the front of one of the letters snags my attention before I can put the lid back in place.

My fingers trail over the letter, plucking it from its place.

I turn it over in my palm and realize the letter's never been opened.

"Hey, Kai," I call over to him.

"Yeah?" he asks, making his way around the coffee table to sit beside me on the worn couch with cigarette burns littering the woven fabric. I hand him the letter addressed to *Malakai Davis.*

He sucks in a breath, his pupils dilating and nostrils flaring.

"What the fuck?" he mutters, running a finger over the return address.

Jamal Davis.

"Who's Jamal?" I ask.

His eyes flit up to meet mine. "*My father.*"

I hold my breath, unsure of what to say.

To Kai's knowledge, his dad left him and his mom when he was ten without saying a single word about where he was going or how to contact him.

But this?

This doesn't look like he left without a word.

Kai tears into the envelope, pulling a white, lined piece of notebook paper out.

His eyes skim across the letter before he tosses it onto the table, his large hands gripping the side of the box and hoisting it off of my lap and into his.

He frantically starts combing through the letters.

My fingers and toes start to tingle, and my hands feel clammy as I watch and wait to find out what the hell is going on.

Each of the envelopes, of which there must be hundreds, is addressed the same way.

All of them to Kai, and with the same return address.

It doesn't take long before we're sitting beside a pile of opened letters.

Kai sags into the couch cushions, his breaths coming out in short bursts as he stares up at the ceiling.

I don't dare make a sound as he processes whatever this is.

Several strained, long moments slip by before his glassy eyes finally meet mine.

"It was all a lie," he whispers. "He never wanted to leave."

My hand lands on his forearm, squeezing reassuringly.

"She kicked him out, and he's been trying to contact me for years. She told him I didn't want anything to do with him and to leave me alone," he explains. "But he never did," Kai finishes, the words barely a whisper.

He leans forward, covering his face with his hands. "I have to contact him," he finally says, slapping his hands to his thighs before standing abruptly. He reaches down for my hands, pulling me off the couch before gathering all the letters back into the box. I follow him out of the trailer, grabbing a couple of the bags we had filled with trash before chucking them in the dumpster at the corner of the lot while Kai locks up.

The ride back to our apartment is quiet and tense as he processes all of this new information.

Chapter Twenty-Two

Lea

Tuesday, December 24, 2024

"K ai, are you *sure* you're still up for this?" I ask, calling across the apartment to him.

"Yes, Lea! For the hundredth time, I'm good," he says with a chuckle.

The last few days have been strange.

Kai got in contact with Jamal after he'd had a day to cool off from everything. It was awkward as hell, even from where I sat beside him, listening to the strained conversation.

They're having dinner on the twenty-sixth, and I know Kai's been creating a list of things he wants to ask him before he even considers a relationship with the man.

I take a deep, steadying breath as I sit on the edge of my bed, securing the red buckle over my ankle.

When I'm finally ready, I stand, taking a look in the mirror.

My tall, slim frame is covered in thigh-high stockings and a red velvet dress that falls perfectly over my minimal curves. The white faux fur trim hangs from my shoulders and at the hem of the short dress, falling at my mid-thigh.

I make my way into the living room, where Kai is seated on the countertop, wearing a Santa suit and black boots that should be illegal to wear around children.

Or anyone besides me, for that matter.

His muscles ripple against the red velvet of his suit as he dunks a chocolate chip cookie in a glass of milk, bringing it to his lips.

A moan slips out, and his head falls back against the cabinet. "Damn, this chubby fucker was really onto something. Milk and cookies should be a year-round staple," he groans.

"Now, Santa," I chide, wagging my finger at him. His eyes flit across the room, landing on me for the first time since I walked out here. "It's not very nice to call someone a chubby fucker, and *definitely* not very jolly to sit on the counter when you've literally spanked me for doing the same!"

He snorts, and a wry grin spreads across his full lips. "And I look forward to doing it again," he tells me, wiggling his brows before he jumps off the counter, prowling toward me.

He snatches the hats from the kitchen island, shoving his on before he pulls mine over my head, covering my eyes. He grips my hips, dragging me against his firm body as my hands fly to my face, trying to fix the hat.

"How come you look so fucking hot dressed like an old woman whose best friends are literal fucking reindeer?" he asks, chuckling as he leans in to kiss the tip of my nose.

The white fur trim of his suit jacket and hat contrast with his deep-topaz complexion.

I twirl a lock of my platinum hair around my finger, batting my lashes at him playfully. "I don't know, but maybe if you're a good boy"—I bring my lips to the shell of his ear—"I'll let you unwrap me later."

A deep groan passes his lips. Kai thrusts into me, and I can't help the airy giggle that slips free. "You're trying to kill me, angel," he grunts.

"Nope," I tell him, my eyes flicking to the clock above the stove. "But your coach might if we're late." I pull out of his grasp and swat his firm, round ass as I saunter past him. "Come on, Santa, let's get a move on," I joke.

I hear him grumble behind me, and I know he's following me when I make it down the first set of stairs outside and hear the door shut and lock above me.

Chapter Twenty-Three

Kai

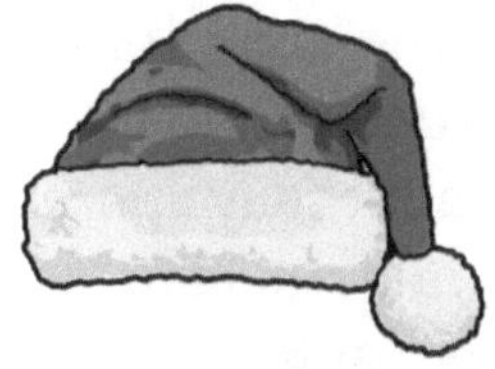

Lea's pink cheeks and wide smile lit up all night as we sat in a large conference room, handing out donated gifts to the kids here for the hospital.

My heart aches to know that many of them are here without their parents for the holidays. This hospital is a well-known children's cancer center, and wanting their kids to have the best shot at recovery, there are things these parents have had to compromise on as a result.

Growing up with a mom who could never hold down a job because of her mental illness, and what I thought was an absentee father who skipped out on his family, I know just a taste of what some of these kids must be feeling.

I learned that there's at least a handful whose parents tried to stay as long as they could. Without a job and the new year bringing with it a fresh start to their insurance deductibles, it just wasn't possible to be here, especially not in New York, where it's disgustingly expensive this time of year.

Lea claps her hands excitedly after she puts the book down that she'd been reading to the kids, and when I look out across the room, I can tell they're all as enraptured with her as I am.

Lea is stunning. No matter what she's wearing or how messy her hair is, she's got this way of lighting up a whole damn room, and I have no idea how I've gone this long without fully appreciating that.

The kids continue to clap as Lea grasps my hand in hers, squeezing gently. Her bright-white teeth gleam under the harsh fluorescence, that one slightly crooked canine of hers standing out among her other, perfectly straight teeth.

My heart hammers in my chest, and my pulse climbs as realization starts to hit me. Before I can even think of the words, Jaclyn, the nurse manager who coordinated this evening, approaches us with a large smile.

"Hey, guys, thanks again for doing this! The kids really seemed to enjoy themselves," she says happily.

"No problem at all," I say, looking over to Lea. "It was actually pretty fun."

"I had a great time," Lea tells her.

Jaclyn presses her lips together, squinting one eye and shrugging her shoulders in a mixture of guilt and nerves. "Would you guys mind making just a couple more stops before you head out for the night? A few of the really sick kids weren't able to make it out here due to precautions their providers have had to set in place because of their immuno-compromised status, but we don't want them to miss out entirely," she explains.

"Oh my gosh, of course not!" Lea tells her, standing abruptly and dragging me with her as she grasps my hand in hers.

Jaclyn blows out a sigh, her shoulders relaxing. "Really?" she asks, hope lacing her words. "You two are incredible," she tells us. But she's wrong. *Lea* is incredible, and I'm just trying to catch up so I can be worthy of her one day.

Chapter Twenty-Four
Lea

Even with a blue-and-white surgical mask on, I can still tell Kai has a wide grin on his handsome face as he sits beside a little girl named Khushi.

She's a witty little spitfire, and it's clear that she has no interest in letting cancer get her down.

Her parents sit on the opposite side of her bed, their heads resting against each other; the bags under their eyes and tired smiles tug at my heartstrings. I can't even begin to imagine how much this family has gone through, but I can only hope for better days ahead.

A knock raps against the door, drawing our attention to where Jaclyn is popping her head into the room. "Hey, I think it's time for Santa and Mrs. Claus to head out so they can make it to all the other children around the world," she says.

Khushi leans back in her bed, crossing her arms across her chest. She rolls her eyes dramatically as she says, "I'm *ten*, Miss Jacky. I know Santa doesn't exist."

The room fills with laughter, and when it quiets down, Kai's eyes are filled with unshed tears.

Khushi reaches out for Kai's hand, holding it beside her, and for the first time since we met her nearly an hour ago, a twinge of sadness is evident in her glassy eyes. "In my culture, we have a saying, 'eopjilleojin murida', which means don't cry over slurped water," she says, turning to look at her parents. "Right?" she asks them to clarify.

They chuckle, and her dad leans forward, resting his forearms on the thin mattress. "Don't cry over *spilled* water," he emphasizes. "It's just like the American saying 'don't cry over spilled milk,' meaning there's no use in crying over what's already happened."

Khushi nods exaggeratedly. "Mhmm, so don't cry for me because I might be sick now, but I won't be forever." Confidence exudes from her tiny body.

Kai squeezes her fingers. "I have *every* confidence that you're right. You," he says, pointing a long finger at her, "are a fighter." He looks over at me, his eyes crinkling at the sides. "And Mrs. Claus and I'll be cheering you on from the North Pole," he jokes, shooting her a wide, goofy smile to clear the tension from the room.

Khushi's bright smile returns, and she extends her arms out for a hug from each of us. Kai's reluctance to leave her is almost palpable as they wave goodbye to each other.

Jaclyn walks us out of the hospital, thanking us profusely for staying, and we volunteer to do it again next year.

This is a holiday tradition I can get behind.

Chapter Twenty-Five
Kai

My chest feels heavy as we make our way home, but as we pass the rink, I make a split-second decision.

I cut a U-turn, heading back there as Lea straightens in her seat. "Kai, what are you doing?"

"Going skating," I tell her because for as long as I can remember, being on the ice is the only thing that's managed to consistently improve my mood.

She says nothing as I park in the spot closest to the doors, not wanting her out in the snow with just those tights to cover her legs.

She grasps my hand as we stand at the door, her body curling into me for warmth. "Kai, how do you know the code to get in here?" she hisses at me when the light on the lock turns green, signaling we're free to go inside.

I chuckle beside her. "Don't worry about it."

She shoots daggers at me, suspicion running rampant. I flip the switch for the lights that illuminate the ice, leaving the rest of the rink in darkness.

"Consider it a Christmas miracle," I joke, ignoring her scowl.

We each head toward the locker rooms to find our skates and meet back out on the ice.

Lea looks adorable in her little red dress, her pearlescent waves flowing around her face as she takes over the ice in her bulky black skates.

They're certainly not the pretty white ones the ice skaters wear, but I think these suit her better anyway.

She waves me over to her, and when I'm close enough, she takes off past me, leaving a spray of ice in her wake.

I shake my head, laughter flowing through me as I watch her in amazement.

She has this way of always bringing me out of my head, of allowing me to feel every one of the emotions warring inside me. Even when I was busy pretending I didn't like her, she never made me feel like I was less than for having such strong feelings.

Her smile is wistful as she dances circles around me in the center of the ice, and my breath gets stuck in my throat.

My lips part, and I work on a swallow as my knees feel weak.

This gorgeous, incredible woman has been just within reach my whole life, and had I even stopped to let myself realize how amazing she is, maybe I could've avoided wasting so many years spent without her by my side.

Because, Lea? She's the kind of woman who'll have you on your knees for her, in more than one way, begging for even a morsel of her attention. And somehow, I'm lucky enough to have her eyes fully on me.

I pump my legs, carrying my body across the ice and over to her. My arms wrap around her, spinning us in small circles as she tosses her head back, laughter ringing through the rink.

With Lea in my arms, it feels like I'm hyperaware of every cell in my body. Each and every one of them completely drawn to her, honed in on her responses.

She grips my cheeks in her cold hands, staring into my eyes with a small smile before her lips connect with mine.

We have never kissed.

We've done all sorts of things with and to each other, but never have my lips been on hers.

Just as I'd expect, they're soft and pliant under mine, and a low moan rumbles through my chest in response to the tiny gasp she releases. I swipe my tongue along the seam of her lips, pleading for entrance, and when she opens, my tongue dives in.

That sugar cookie scent of hers surrounds me, filling my lungs, and the same sweetness hits my tongue when hers connects with mine. It's like a shock to my system as I come to realize that Lea, through all her imperfections, is somehow still perfect. *To me* anyway.

And I *fully* intend to show her that tonight, and every night from here on out.

Chapter Twenty-Six

Lea

Tuesday, December 24, 2024

Kai's lips sear into mine, his hot tongue lapping at my mouth as he runs his fingers over my ass and down the back of my thighs. He hoists me up his body, our mouths still connected as his blades slide across the ice.

My fingers dig into his shoulders, the kiss taking on a feverish quality as his raspy moans fill my mouth.

When he finally pulls away, he's panting, mouth slightly ajar as he steps off the ice and into the penalty box.

A shiver skates down my spine, and a wanton cry leaves my throat as Kai sits on the bench, twisting my body so my ass is in his lap. His thick cock presses against my center.

Kai's hands trail under my dress, his fingers looping in the waist of my bright-red panties before dragging them down.

"I plan to worship every inch of your delicious body tonight," he says, exposing my ass and pressing a warm kiss to one cheek. "But until I can get you home and in my bed, this'll have to do," he says, pulling himself out and stroking his shaft before lining himself up with my center.

He grips my hips tightly in his large hands after he's worked the tip of his cock into me.

I wet my lips, the periphery of my vision getting hazy as I slowly sink down on him. The idea of being *here*, where we work our bodies to the bone, playing the game we love while doing *this*, feels so much more intimate than when we're at home.

Goosebumps line my skin, and my legs wobble as I try to remain upright.

"Hands on your knees, angel, lean forward, and give me a good view of this pretty ass." Kai groans behind me.

I work down the saliva pooling in my mouth, placing my trembling hands on my unsteady knees as I sink down onto him until I'm fully seated.

I cry out as Kai moans, the empty rink echoing the sounds of our cries back at us.

"Come on, baby, give me one good one, and then I'll take you home and we can take our time," he says, using his hands on my sides to guide me up and down his length.

"I don't—" I whimper. "It's just too—"

He increases his pace, his moans and mine inter-mingling and becoming more rapid as I take every inch of him to the hilt.

"You're such a good girl, Lea. And you know what they say about good girls around the holidays?" he asks, but I can barely focus on his words as my thighs shake and my pussy lips slide along him.

I manage to shake my head, words escaping me. "What—" I groan when he slips the pads of his fingers around my front, rubbing them against my needy clit. "What do they say?"

He slams his hips into me, my hands slipping off of my knees and his arms the only thing holding me up. He wraps his arms under my thighs, spreading me wide and taking on all of my weight. "They say," he whispers against the shell of my ear, dropping my feet back to the ground. My fingers grip the wall just beneath the plexiglass as Kai stands up behind me, covering my folded frame with his own. "Good girls get gifts, and Santa's about to make one very special good girl come all over his dick."

And just like that, a few more thrusts send me careening over the edge. I'm a whimpering mess in his arms as he fills me with his cum, calling out my name as he does.

"Lea, oh *fuck*, Lea," he moans. "Yes, baby, so fuck-ing good."

We're gasping for air as he sits back down on the bench, taking my body with his and keeping me close to his chest. He buries his face in my hair, and for the first time in a long time, I feel like I'm really, truly safe.

My muscles are completely spent and relaxed as we lay in Kai's bed after my *fourth* orgasm of the night.

"A very merry Christmas Eve indeed," Kai says, shaking the bed with his deep chuckle.

I can't help the snort that slips free as I roll onto my side, propping a leg over Kai's and wrapping my arm around his waist.

"I'm exhausted," I tell him, a huge yawn choosing that moment to present itself.

Kai's smile widens. He presses a kiss to my cheek, smoothing a hand over my tousled hair and pulling his comforter over us.

"Goodnight, angel."

"Goodnight, Santa," I say with a repressed giggle, and he pinches my ass cheek before we both doze off.

Chapter Twenty-Seven

Kai

Wednesday, December 25, 2024

I wake up with the smell of vanilla sugar cookies surrounding me and Lea's long white hair draped over my chest, her warm body snuggled into mine.

A smile curves my lips as she peers up at me through long, pale lashes. "Morning," she whispers, her voice full of sleep.

"Good morning, angel. Merry Christmas," I tell her, pressing a kiss to the top of her head.

She smiles brightly at me, sitting up and stretching her arms over her head. I hear the pop in her back as it cracks with the movement.

When she's done stretching, Lea climbs on top of me, wrapping her limbs around me. My hands skim down to her ass, clutching her firmly against my body as I gaze up at her pretty face. "You're gorgeous, angel," I tell her, my tone reverent.

A light pink colors her cheeks and chest, and I can't help but tease her, craving any and every response she'll give me. *The good and the bad.* "And your dentist deserves a raise. If I hadn't been there, I wouldn't even know you've got veneers for those teeth you'd practically lost from that puck to the face," I say, smirking.

She rolls her eyes. "You can't ever just be *sweet* for a moment, can you?"

I tilt my head, and my eyes crinkle at the sides as I try to hold back my smile. "Of course I can. You tell me I'm sweet all the time. Like when I'm eating your pussy, and don't forget just how *sweet* my cum is when it's dripping down your throat." I smile innocently, and she smacks a hand to my chest, rolling her eyes as she climbs out of bed, and like the foolish man that I am, I follow her on instinct. Now that she's embedded herself into my soul, I can't seem to leave her alone, even if she wanted me to.

She grabs a pair of sweats and a t-shirt, tossing them at my face. I catch them and change as she works a pair of my gym shorts up her legs, tying the string tight and rolling the waistband so they don't fall to her feet. She then steals another one of my shirts, one I'm sure I'll never get back, but what's mine is hers, and if I really allow myself to think back on this, it has been for a while.

My heart included.

"You want pancakes for breakfast?" I ask her, following her to my bedroom door.

She scoffs at me over her shoulder, her fingers curling around the doorknob. "*Absolutely not.* Pancakes are nothing more than waffles' soggy, floppy, and *sad* counterparts. Besides, the pockets are perfect for—" Her words are cut off as we enter the living room to find lights hanging over the windows, a massive Christmas tree decorated in the corner, and a menorah with blue candles sitting in the center of the coffee table.

Neither of us are even Jewish; what the shit is going on?

And since I know it sure as shit wasn't *Santa* who came down our chimney last night to decorate, my eyes swing across the living room, landing on *Liam.*

His face is as red as Rudolph's nose as he bolts off the couch, clenched fists at his sides as he stomps over to me.

Lea watches with a wide-eyed stare and gaping mouth as her brother pushes me into the wall. I manage to catch myself before I can trip and fall on my ass.

"Woah, dude, what the fuck?" I ask, shocked as hell that Liam, my annoyingly calm best friend, has apparently had a flip switch in his brain at the sight of his sister and I leaving my room *together.*

"Are you fucking kidding me, Malakai? You're supposed to be my *best friend,* and I find you hooking up with my sister? You couldn't keep it in your pants for a fucking month?" His words drip with venom as he shoots daggers into me.

My eyes flit nervously to Lea, whose surprised expression is wiped clean. A new, indifferent one has taken its place as she sits back into the couch cushions, propping her legs up and resting her arms behind her head.

Liam snaps his fingers in front of my face. "Hey, fuck face, eyes on me, motherfucker. Don't fucking look at her," he shouts, spit flying out of his mouth, making me cringe.

"Jesus, dude, you're acting like a rabid animal," I tell him. "Get a fucking grip, and don't forget, *you're the reason she's even here.*"

His head rears back, eyes widening a fraction. "She's *here* because you *both* needed a roommate. She's not your little fuck toy," he tells me as if I'm not already fully fucking aware.

She's so much more.

My eyes never fully leave Lea, so I don't miss the subtle eye roll she directs at him.

Crossing my arms over my chest, I straighten my spine, fully prepared to take a hit to my pretty face today. For Lea, I refuse to back down to him.

"You don't think I fucking *know that?* Your sister's incredible, and she somehow manages to make me smile even on my worst days. She's so goddamn thoughtful, and always puts others ahead of her own needs, which you'd fucking *know* if you got your head out of your ass."

He squints his eyes at me, some of his bravado leaving with each breath he takes.

His lips pinch when he looks over at Lea, still lying on the couch, watching the show unfold before her.

"What is he talking about, Lea?"

She waves a hand in the air, remaining as nonchalant as possible before she says, "It's nothing, Liam."

"Don't give me that shit, Lea. You've been hiding things from me, and I think it's time we get it all out in the open."

Jesus fucking Christ, I hope like hell we *do not* do *that*.

I see her throat bob as she swallows, finally sitting up. "My migraine meds are just really expensive, and I didn't want to worry you. I know you've been sending money to Mom and Dad since you signed with the Scarlets," she admits, and my chest heaves a small sigh that she left out the part where she, no, *we* create porn for people online to jack off to so she can afford the simple luxury of not having an ice pick jabbed into her skull.

His eyes swing to me, pinning me with a glare. "You knew about this and didn't tell me?"

I roll my eyes. "Lea's a big girl. She can disclose whatever the hell she wants to you. Or not." I shrug. "It's not my business."

He shoots me another glare before looking back to Lea. "I'm making *more* than enough money now, Lea. I'm sure I can help with the cost of your meds!"

"They're twenty-three hundred dollars a month," she deadpans.

I watch as all the blood drains from his face. "Shit, Lea, I'm sorry. I—" he stammers. "I hadn't realized it was that expensive, but I promise you, I *have the money now*. I just got my sign-on bonus, and the money I'm making is literally pouring in. I'm still living in a shitty studio apartment because I don't want to splurge until I have a fat savings account, but *please* just let me take this burden on for you."

Her big, puppy dog eyes are glassy as she stands from the couch, wrapping her arms around her brother's waist. He squeezes her tightly to him, and she rests her chin on his shoulder before speaking to him in a quiet, watery voice.

"Hey, Liam," she mutters.

"Yes, Lea?" he asks, his voice weary.

"I think I'm falling for your best friend," she tells him, but her eyes are on me the whole time.

I hear Liam suck air between his teeth, but I pay him little mind. My chin falls to my chest, a wide grin splitting across my face the moment I recover, and I resist the urge to pump my fucking fist in the air like some clown. I feel exhilarated, endorphins flooding my body, a tingling sensation overcoming each of my nerve fibers.

"Fuck yeah!" I finally say, unable to hold it in any longer, and when my eyes meet hers, I tell her the truth. "The feeling's mutual, angel."

"I hate you both," Liam whispers, and I can't help the laugh that slips past my lips. Lea releases him, doubling forward and choking on her own laugh. "This really isn't funny," he says, rolling his eyes and crossing his arms over his chest. "But it's Christmas, so I guess I'll learn to live with your *very poor decision-making skills.*"

Lea recovers from her laughing fit, smacking Liam over the back of the head and waltzing into the kitchen. "Any chance you put a waffle maker under that tree?" she calls out to Liam.

"As a matter of fact..."

Chapter Twenty-Eight

Lea

My cheeks hurt by the time we're done with brunch. Liam's inability to hold a grudge against anyone, especially Kai, works in our favor.

They'd been picking on each other for the last hour, and despite the fact that Kai had his own stack of chocolate chip waffles, which he topped with whipped cream and red and green sprinkles, he still happily ate from *my* plate.

If this is what relationships are like, I can understand why so many marriages end in divorce. Whoever I marry better keep their paws off my food.

Though, from the looks of it, that won't be happening.

The three of us are crammed into the tiny living room, Liam sitting on the floor by the Christmas tree because, apparently, it was *too soon* to see me sit in Kai's lap so Liam could avoid sitting on the hard floor.

But if he's gonna be a baby about it, so be it.

"If you really think we're gonna let you go over there alone, you're dead wrong," Liam tells Kai with a laugh.

"Come on, man. It'll be awkward as hell, and if you two come, that'll only be amplified."

Liam rolls his eyes, crossing his arms over his chest. "You act as if we haven't already met the guy. He's your *dad*, Kai. Our parents still live in the piece of shit apartment we grew up in before you and your mom moved to the trailer."

Kai's eyes land on me, the soft crinkle around them telling me that he wants saving, but unfortunately for him, I agree with Liam. "Kai, I think Liam's right. It'll be awkward either way, but if we go with you, at least you'll have some more support." I reach across the loveseat to take his hands in mine, squeezing them gently. "We *want* to be there for you," I tell him, my voice a hushed whisper.

He closes his eyes for a moment before meeting mine again, bringing our hands up to his mouth to press a soft kiss along my knuckles. "Okay, you can come."

Liam, always one for the dramatics, claps his hands excitedly. "Hell yeah!" he says with a little "whoop."

Through the speakers, *How The Grinch Stole Christmas* plays on TV, with the narrator reaching the part about the Grinch's heart growing three sizes that day.

Having Kai, this man I've had a reluctant crush on for the majority of my life, in our tiny, albeit cozy, apartment, my brother beside us, my best friend, and her fiancé on the way definitely leaves me feeling like *my* heart is growing at least three sizes.

I smirk over at Kai, a memory popping into my head. "You know, I still can't believe you managed to keep your full name a secret," I tell him.

Liam's shoulders shake with laughter. "He sure as shit couldn't get away with making fun of *your* name if you'd known." Liam voices the same thought I had.

Kai raises his arms, his palms facing me. "Hey now," he drawls. "I never said I was making fun of your name! I'm merely emphasizing every letter," he says, smirking.

Liam, the shit-stirrer he sometimes is, leans back against the wall beside the fully lit tree. "Oh no, he was *absolutely* talking crap."

I grab a pillow from behind me, chucking it at his face, but of course, his reflexes are entirely too fast, and he catches it and tucks it behind his back.

"Alright, children," Kai says, standing and smacking his hands on his thighs. "It's Christmas Day, which means we have cookies to bake and Chinese food to order."

I roll my eyes at him. "In case you haven't noticed our barren cabinets, we don't *have* anything to make cookies."

He dramatically opens two cabinet doors, the ones just to the right of the one that contains all of his not-so-hidden peanut butter-filled snacks.

My jaw nearly hits the floor, and my eyes suddenly feel misty. "Think again, angel. We have cookie supplies for days. Besides, it *is* your favorite holiday, isn't it?"

Liam looks between us, his head turning side to side, almost comically. "How in the ever-loving-fuck did we get here, people? Come on! I leave you guys for less than a month and you're already at this level of annoyingly adorable? It's disgusting," he says, tossing his hands up as he storms off to what used to be his room. "I'm gonna take a leak. You guys better get all your mushy feelings out before I get back," he huffs.

I round the kitchen island, wrapping my arms around Kai's shoulders. He crushes me to his warm body, and my head spins, my hands clutching his cheeks. I press a gentle kiss to his soft, full lips.

"Thank you," I whisper, my voice watery.

He plants another kiss on my lips before reluctantly releasing me as my bedroom door creaks open. "Anything for you, angel," he whispers back as Liam pulls out a stool, taking a seat at the kitchen island.

"I'll oversee the project. You guys can do the actual baking." He taps his fingers on the counter. "And don't worry, I'll do my part to clean up," he says, winking playfully at Kai.

"Licking the spoon and leaving it in the sink for me to clean and *you* to get salmonella is *not* cleaning up," I say, rolling my eyes.

The rest of the day passes in a complete blur of baking cookies, Liam eating so many that he looked green for the better part of the day, and Mona's never-ending love for Americanized Chinese food leading to a competition between her and Kai over who could eat more.

It came as absolutely no surprise that the winner, by a landslide, was Mona.

When everyone's either in my room or on the loveseat sleeping, Kai and I head to his bedroom.

A mistletoe now hangs in the doorway, and I look up at it, squinting before turning back to him. "When'd you put this here?" I ask.

He shrugs. "I didn't," he whispers, but a smile stretches his lips as he reaches out for me, tugging us underneath it. "But why waste a perfectly good opportunity for a kiss, Leonora?" he says with a smirk.

I roll my eyes, wrapping my hands around his neck, and stand up on my tiptoes, pressing my lips to his. Tiny sparks fly between us, and my heart rate speeds up.

He lifts me and carries me to bed, dropping me in the center before climbing in behind me.

Kai's strong arms are wrapped around me, and I've never felt so safe.

In just a few short weeks, I've gotten to know him better than I had in the twenty-six years we'd known each other. *That alone feels like a holiday miracle.*

Chapter Twenty-Nine

Kai

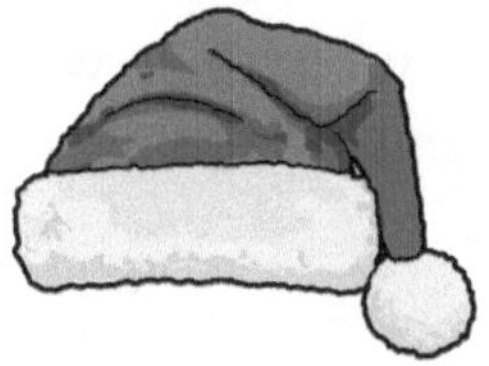

Thursday, December 26, 2024

My hands have stopped shaking, but my leg still occasionally bounces under the long wooden table as we sit with assorted desserts sprawled out in front of us.

Having Lea and Liam seated on either side of me helps settle my nerves, but I still can't shake the anxiety at being in this home with a little sister and stepmom I hadn't even known existed. Not only that, but I haven't seen my father since I was *ten*. Nothing about this situation is reassuring at first glance, but they've all been unbelievably welcoming since the moment I stepped through the doors with two guests I hadn't even remembered to ask about bringing.

I don't think there's anything that could accurately explain the way I'm feeling right now as I look across the table, my eyes set on my father, a man I spent most of my life believing had walked out on me. A man who I resemble in so many ways.

The reality of having grown up in a home with a mom who, maybe even unknowingly, perpetuated the harmful, disturbing, and downright *wrong* stereotype that Black men walk out on their children doesn't evade me. Because of her, I missed out on seventeen years with a man who could've helped me handle my teenage years better, who could've made me feel *safe* in my own skin.

For years, I've thought he simply hadn't wanted me or my mom. I felt unloved and unwanted for so much of my childhood that it carried through my adulthood too. And as much as I want to be angry, hell, I *wish* I could feel the resentment I know most people would, I just *can't*.

Because at the end of the day, when I think about my mom, my mind is filled with the years she spent battling a mental health condition that she was never equipped to fight. And through it all, she somehow managed to fill our crappy, tiny trailer with love and laughter when her mind was clear enough. So instead, I'm holding onto the thought that she really had believed she was doing the right thing when she kicked him out and that maybe she regrets it too.

"I don't tell you this because I want you to resent your mom," Jamal, my *dad*, says, a small line drawn between his bushy brows. "I just want you to know that it wasn't my choice."

I nod, unable to say anything just yet, so he continues.

"We were young when we had you, but we were in love, and being with your mother is something I'll never regret." He looks over to his wife, Jazmine, their hands clasped together over the red-and-gold tablecloth. "But I firmly believe that everything happens for a reason, Malakai. When she kicked me out, I had no idea she was dealing with psychosis," he says, hanging his head. "It wasn't like a switch had flipped overnight. There was a slow progression of things. She started coming home at weird times, we'd get into arguments because she wouldn't tell me where she was, and I had no way of explaining where she had run off to to our *son*. As weeks went on like that, things continued to get worse between us. When she told me to leave, I thought we'd take a break, cool off, and work things out. Then, you were both gone when I showed up to our apartment a week later after not hearing anything from her. I managed to find the address online after she *finally* decided to register to vote," he says, shaking his head, his lips upturned with a small grin.

"She never actually cast her vote though," I admit, chuckling lightly. It's not really funny, but it's definitely on brand for her.

"Of course she didn't," he says, his laughter a deep hearty sound.

The smile falls from my face as questions start to flood my mind. "Why didn't you come back for me?"

"Kai, I tried. I promise, I did. But I couldn't afford a lawyer, and frankly, the chances of a Black man who wasn't in the best financial situation winning custody over a white woman who at least owned her trailer, well, they were slim. And I've got no interest in changing the color of my skin, but my financial situation was something I could change, so I did. I worked every day with you motivating me, to be better and more successful than the day before, and when I finally had a home, a car, *assets*, things I could use to convince a judge to give me a shot, I realized you were an adult," he says, his voice quieting with every word. "Every week, I've sent you a letter, catching you up on my life and your sister's. And every week, I haven't heard a single thing." He pins me with his brown eyes, the same shade of coffee as mine. "Until now."

All the air is sucked out of my lungs as it dawns on me the incredibly specific chain of events that had to happen in order to get me here for this exact moment.

Jazmine squeezes his hand, her pretty light-brown eyes settling on me. She gives me a small, reassuring smile before she says something that has the potential to change everything for me.

"Kai, your father and I spoke in the kitchen after dinner, and we wanted to run something by you," she says, and my stomach starts to tumble with anxiety.

Again, a nod is all I manage, my mouth too dry to speak even if I knew what to say. I feel Lea's hand resting in my lap, and it anchors me as she squeezes my thigh gently.

"It's true that I didn't know she was struggling with schizophrenia," he tells me, his eyes peering over at Jazmine, and when she nods, he continues.

"But she was my partner, and I should've known there was more to it than her suddenly wanting me out of your lives. I should've done more to figure out what was going on, and frankly, I know that'll eat me up inside for a long time, but I want to do something to make peace with it, and I sincerely hope it helps you too."

My brows pinch as I watch my father, his eyes cast downward to his lap. "I'd like to cover the cost of her stay at the psychiatric hospital. I want her to get the help she needs, and I don't want it to be any more of a burden than it's already been for you your whole life."

Air refuses to fill my lungs as I stare at him, un-blinking while my mind tries to pick apart his words. I'm not in a place to say no to him, and frankly, I don't want to.

I want to live a typical life with Lea by my side, not fucking her for a bunch of horny creeps behind a screen to make ends meet, and I want my mom to have access to the care she needs so she can get back to the fun-loving, free-spirited woman I only saw glimpses of growing up.

"Thank you," I breathe out.

He reaches across the table to take my hand, look-ing me in the eye as he says, "Thank *you* for giving me a chance to explain. I wouldn't have blamed you if you'd read my letters and never bothered with me, but I'll continue to spend every day proving to you and your sister that my love for you is unconditional, and no amount of time could erase that."

Unyielding relief. *That* is what I feel. Knowing that I suddenly have a solid support system and an opportunity to get to know the man who makes up this other half of me that I've never understood, it's overwhelming, but in the best way.

"Thank you so much for having us," Lea tells my dad and Jazmine. "Dinner was incredible, and I know this must be such a huge relief for you." She looks back at me, rubbing the pad of her thumb across the inside of my wrist. "Everyone," she finishes, her words sounding choked, and her eyes turn glossy.

I pull her into my side, crushing my arm around her waist to anchor her physically and emotionally.

"You have no idea," my dad answers. "It was great to meet you, and I hope to see you all very soon."

As we leave the home that now represents new opportunities and growth for every aspect of my life, I feel my heart swell in my chest.

Fuck, I'm so damn thankful.

Epilogue: Kai

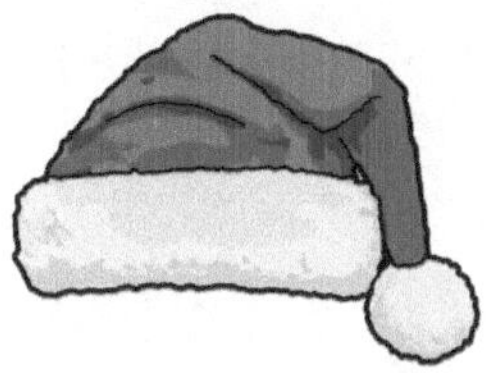

Thursday, July 10, 2025

"**A**nd may we raise a glass to our favorite love-birds! Congratulations to the happy couple, and may you make the right decision on who your best man will be!" Liam says, raising his beer up high as he stands in the center of the private dining room my dad booked at Lea's favorite French bistro.

"To Lea and Kai!" Liam shouts, and everyone follows.

"To Lea and Kai!"

I wrap my arm around Lea's shoulders, pulling her into my side and pressing a kiss above her temple.

Liam takes his seat across from us, crossing his arms on top of the table and leaning in. "I'm still shocked she said yes. I totally thought she'd fuck with you and say no." He chuckles.

Lea rolls her eyes at him, but a sly grin twists her pretty pink lips. "I thought about it," she admits, chuckling.

Lea's mom, Lorelei, mimics her eye roll and says, "I'm still shocked this is even a thing, but I couldn't be happier for you two."

Her dad, Andrew, agrees, smiling brightly at me. "The way you two fought your whole childhoods, I guess we should've known there was something there, but you two were always just so damn mean to each other, we figured it couldn't have been flirting."

"It wasn't," we say in unison, and my dad and Jazmine chuckle along with her parents.

The rest of the night goes on in a blur of my dad practically begging Lea's parents to share stories of our childhood with him, and just like I'd thought, they do exactly that. Getting to see how damn proud my dad looks as they talk about me growing up fills the gaps in my chest I hadn't really thought were still present after Lea had given me the greatest gift by agreeing to marry me.

Fuck, I love this woman.

"How's your mom doing?" Dad asks.

I give him a small smile, and gratitude fills my chest again and again. I'll never be able to thank him enough for the gift he's given me. My mom and I have a long way to go, but thanks to him, we actually have the time to mend the pieces of our relationship she'd fractured.

"She's doing really good, actually. Sticking with her meds, and she's home, but has a nurse come by every morning to help her out around the trailer and make sure she's staying on track."

"I'm glad to hear it. You think she'll be able to make it to the wedding?" he asks, and his bright eyes look hopeful.

"Speaking of which, have you guys set a wedding date yet?" Lorelei asks, giving me an out if I want it.

She's always been good at doing that.

Except this time, I don't want the out. I'm thrilled as hell to be able to answer this one.

My dad's a good man. Better than I could've ever hoped, and getting to know him these last few months has helped me come to terms with so many things I'd previously questioned about my worth. Dad wants to see my mom get better and for her to be a part of my wedding because he knows it's important to me. He still cares about her, and it shows. It's not in the way I imagine he had when they were still together, and definitely not the same as his love for Jazmine, but he wants the best for her.

"We're getting married on Christmas Eve, and I'm pretty sure Mom will be there," I say, though we still plan to volunteer at the hospital like we'd agreed to last year. My throat constricts as a wave of emotions hits me like a high tide.

"Oh my gosh, so romantic!" Mona all but screeches from her end of the table.

Lea laughs quietly beside me. "I'm not sure I'd call it romantic," she admits, averting her gaze to where our hands are intertwined in her lap. "We just wanted to deter as many people as possible from coming since we really only want you guys there," she admits.

"On brand for you guys," Mona says.

We all spend the rest of the night eating and talking, and it really hits me: I'm surrounded by all but one of the most important people in my life, and I genuinely couldn't be happier.

And more than that, *I finally feel like I deserve it all.*

Epilogue: Lea

As if Kai and I being drafted for the same co-ed NHL team wasn't already a fucking miracle, a long-lost aunt of my mom's passed away and left her *everything*. My parents have lived frugally my entire life, and getting to see them ditch their shitty jobs, and move to be closer to Liam, Kai, and me is more than I could have ever imagined for my future.

And now, sitting in my favorite restaurant surrounded by my favorite people, my heart feels like it'll explode with joy and gratitude.

They say you can't pick your family, but if I had to do it all over again with the option of picking, I wouldn't change a single thing. My friends, parents, brother, and of course, my *fiancé* are the most special people, and I'm so blessed to have them in my world.

I can't wait for what the future holds for us.

Extended Epilogue: Kai

Wednesday, December 24, 2025

"**S**he attributes her newfound health to your visit, so it's the least we could do," Khushi's dad tells me.

"Wow, big words coming from a kid who was adamant that Santa wasn't real," I say, smirking down at Khushi, whose straight black hair is trimmed into a bob with a red headband that matches her black suit with red lapels and the red berries dangling from the mistletoe boutonniere pinned to her breast pocket.

"Yeah, and I stand by that," Khushi says, rolling her eyes. "Now, are you gonna marry her, or what? I don't have all day, *Santa.*"

"Damn kid, you're pushy tonight," I say, chuckling as we line up at the end of the aisle behind where Liam's standing with a basket in hand. Music starts to play, and he's off. He struts down the aisle, twirling as he tosses red rose petals with a flourish. He drops down into a low squat before popping back up and shoving tiny bottles of liquor into the waiting hands of our friends and family.

When he makes it to the end, it's our turn.

"As your best man, I'm gonna tell you that I'm glad you didn't pick *him*," she says, practically sneering at Liam. The kid is fucking ridiculous, but Lea and I have grown to love her. After she got the all-clear from her oncologist, her parents called to let us know she was in remission and made sure we knew that it was Khushi who demanded we were told.

"I'm glad I didn't pick his dumbass, either," I tell her, and she smiles a big, missing-toothed one up at me. She grabs my hand and drags me to the end of the aisle where we wait for Lea.

When she appears in her long white gown with red lace overlaying the top half, my heart grows another three sizes in my chest.

Maybe everyone does have their own angel watching over them. And if that's true, I'm fully convinced that Lea is *mine*.

The end.

Afterword

I always incorporate mental health and/or chronic illness representation in my books, and even though this is a novella, and I've got less of a word count to work with, it's no different. Though I'm sure some of you are probably wondering why I chose schizophrenia as such a major topic and in a smutty holiday romance, no less.

The answer is this: Schizophrenia is far more common than most people would believe, and it impacts the lives of so many, but especially around the holidays. It's an illness that can leave you feeling alone in the battle and low on the resources necessary to combat it. The holidays can be a joyful, uplifting time, but they can also be a time that leaves some people feeling more alone than ever. And as I previously mentioned in the foreword, I grew up with someone very near and dear to my heart who struggled with schizophrenia, and while she is a Black woman and Kai's mom is white, that was done on purpose given the other content covered in this book.

I've spent a pretty significant amount of time volunteering in street medicine (providing healthcare to those who are experiencing homelessness), and while I can't speak on behalf of everyone who's experienced homelessness in some form, statistically, mental illness is the number one contributing factor. And more than that, mental illness with a lack of resources. So for this holiday season, I wanted to speak on a topic that impacts 1% of the overall US population but is documented in over 20% of those experiencing homelessness in the US.

Like any mental illness, schizophrenia can leave you feeling hopeless and without support. While no one in this book experiences homelessness, it's a reality for so many, especially around the holidays, which is a major reason it's such a hot topic of discussion this time of year. Paychecks are already spread thin, housing is difficult to come by, and the weather can be impossible to navigate in cold climates, which is why I chose to incorporate it into this novella.

So if you're living with this mental health condition, know or care for someone who is, have ever experienced homelessness, or just feel even a little alone this holiday season, please know that you're never truly alone. I've included some resources below; please feel free to use any and all of them that apply to you.

And know that choosing to write a Black MC with this illness was done with intention. Black Americans are 2.4 times more likely to experience a diagnosis of schizophrenia when compared to white Americans.

As always, I pay reparations to charities and funds that directly benefit the individuals I am benefiting from by writing stories with people who have a dif-

ferent lived experience than my own. I used to avoid adding this part to my books, and instead, I made the payments without anyone knowing. I did this because I don't want to monetize something that I do because I believe it's the right thing. I don't do this to make it a "selling point" for my books, because it's truly a way for me to give back to the people I'm both representing in my books and profiting from. However, after receiving countless messages from readers asking for ways to help those living with some of the conditions I've written about, I've decided to make it more clear, though again, I won't be slapping any stickers on the front of my books saying "10% of profits from this book go to..."
That said, from the comfort of this page in the back of my book, I'll mention that 10% of the net profits from this book are being paid out to the BIPOC Therapy Fund. I've linked this below as well if you'd like to read about their mission or send a donation yourself.
https://mentalhealthliberation.org/bipoc-therapy-fund/

Some BIPOC
Authors I Adore

& You Should Check Out!

Evelyn Leigh[1]
Cynthia A. Rodriguez[2]
Ruby Rana[3]
Vai Denton[4]
Kennedy Ryan[5]
Marja Graham[6]
Nisha Sharma[7]
Talia Hibbert[8]
Shilo Kino[9]
N.M. Patel[10]
Natasha Bishop[11]
Janisha Boswell[12]
Deanna Grey[13]
J.S. Jasper[14]
Kristina Forest[15]
A.E. Valdez[16]
Miah Onsha[17]
Anna P.[18]
Varsha Chitnis[19]
Amy Oliviera[20]
Siren Crow[21]

Mikayla Hornedo[22]
Layna James[23]
I.B. Solís[24]
Britney S. Lewis[25]

---

1. Evelyn Leigh
2. Cynthia A. Rodriguez
3. Ruby Rana
4. Vai Denton
5. Kennedy Ryan
6. Marja Graham
7. Nisha Sharma
8. Talia Hibbert
9. Shilo Kino
10. N.M. Patel
11. Natasha Bishop
12. Janisha Boswell
13. Deanna Grey
14. J.S. Jasper
15. Kristina Forest
16. A.E. Valdez
17. Miah Onsha
18. Anna P.
19. Varsha Chitnis
20. Amy Oliviera

21. Siren Crow

22. Mikayla Hornedo

23. Layna James

24. I.B. Solís

25. Britney S. Lewis

Acknowledgements

Thank you to my incredible sensitivity readers for making each of my books a reality. Especially to Evelyn Leigh (author of Elevator Pitch) for helping me hone the voices of my Black MCs. While I've spent my life with such an incredibly diverse friend group, I know that I don't understand all the nuances of AAVE and could never accurately portray a Black character on my own without help, nor would I want to. I think people really misunderstand just how much of a group effort publishing books can be. There is so much collaboration throughout, and much like raising a child, it takes a village to "raise" a book baby too. So thank you for your friendship, your unyielding support, and your wisdom. Here's to many, many more books in our futures!

To Annie for sensitivity reading for Khushi and her family. You're wonderful. <3

To Cynthia A. Rodriguez (author of a whole bunch of goodness, including Love Sick and the Second Chance series). Thank you for the time and thoughtfulness you've put into helping ensure this book is in the best shape possible prior to edits, and for your encouragement and friendship.

To Sarah from Hockey Smut Book Club for seeing my vision and agreeing to collaborate on this project as a special edition! You're wonderful in all the ways, and I'm so proud of everything you've accomplished with your page, discord, book club, book box, and so much more to come. They aren't ready for you ;)

To Madi Danielle, who made sure I knew that Chaturbate was, in fact, a real company so that I may now present to you "Mastur-chat." Thanks for not letting me get sued by a porn company! Though that *would* surely be an accomplishment all on its own.

An honorable mention to Kath Richards (author of A Love Most Fatal, aka, my favorite mafia rom-com ever, which you absolutely have to read). She didn't have her hands in this book directly, but she was always there on the sidelines cheering me on. So thank you for that, and thanks for being you <3

About the author

Giuliana Victoria is an author based in Pennsylvania who shares her readers' deep love of all things romance. She's a full-time physician assistant working in gynecology-oncology, and obstetrics, whose passion lies in being there for her patients during their most vulnerable moments, and finding hope where it's hard to find.

When Giuliana isn't writing swoon-worthy book boyfriends, she can be found delivering babies, hiking with her three large breed rescue dogs, and, of course, curled up with a good book beside her husband.

She hopes you'll love **Mistletoe Misconduct** as much as she enjoyed writing it, and she looks forward to sharing all of her future works with her incredible readers.